voices

voices

Sue Mayfield

*Hodder
Children's
Books*

A division of Hodder Headline Limited

A Catalogue record for this book is available from
the British Library

ISBN 0 340 86063 4

Typeset by Avon DataSet Ltd,
Bidford-on-Avon, Warwickshire

Printed and bound in Great Britain by
Bookmarque Ltd, Croydon Surrey

The paper and board used in this paperback are natural
recyclable products made from wood grown in sustainable
forests. The manufacturing processes conform to the
environmental regulations of the country of origin.

Hodder Children's Books
a division of Hodder Headline Limited
338 Euston Road
London NW1 3BH

To Tim, with thanks

Be not afeard; the isle is full of noises,
Sounds, and sweet airs, that give delight
  and hurt not.
Sometimes a thousand twangling
  instruments
Will hum about mine ears . . .

. . . and sometime voices . . .

The Tempest Act III Scene ii

Dramatis Personae

Isabel Bright – a girl in the Lower Sixth
Alice – her sister
Mel – her mum
Pete – her stepdad
Macy Paige – her best friend
Jamie Burrows – her ex-boyfriend
Siobhan – her dance teacher
Mr O'Leary – her singing teacher
Doe Redman – her drama teacher
Cleopatra – her cat
Duncan MacLeod – a chance acquaintance

The Tempest
William Shakespeare

Dramatis Personae

Alonso, King of Naples – Rosie Mason
Sebastian, his brother – Jude Lomax
Prospero, the overthrown Duke of Milan – Sebastian Reeves
Antonio, his brother, now Duke of Milan – Chloe Stretton
Ferdinand, son of the King of Naples – Jamie Burrows
Gonzalo, an honest old councillor – Phil Colvin
Adrian, a Lord – Sara Bottomley
Francisco, another Lord – Jennifer Murphy
Caliban, a savage and deformed slave – Andy Shaw
Trinculo, a jester – Natalie Roberts
Stephano, a drunken butler – Razia Mahmood
Master of a ship – Sonia Bogdanovich
Boatswain – Jenny Murphy
Miranda, daughter of Prospero – Isabel Bright
Ariel, an airy spirit – Macy Paige
Iris – Kirsty Baker
Ceres – Sara Bottomley
Juno – Natalie Roberts
Nymphs and Reapers – Razia Mahmood, Jenny Murphy

Prologue

Enter Isabel stage left. She tears up a photograph and lets the pieces fall to the floor. Turning to the audience, she says:

ISABEL:

Jamie Burrows is a poser and a creep. I don't know what I ever saw in him. He's the most vain, shallow, self-obsessed person on the planet. Not only does he carry a mirror in the back pocket of his jeans but he looks at himself constantly in shop windows, car wing-mirrors and even the backs of spoons. How sad is that? Once, when he was just about to kiss me, I caught him looking at his reflection in my sunglasses! "Just checking that I'm still gorgeous," he said, flashing me his white-toothed boy-band smile.

Apparently, he'd been seeing Kirsty Baker for weeks before he got round to telling me I was dumped. That was bad enough, but it gets worse. He dumped me right in the middle of my GCSEs. Worse still, he didn't even have the guts to tell me to my face. He dumped me by text message. How low is that? It was the night before my History exam. There I was, stuffing my head with the Schlieffen Plan and

1

suffragettes and the Battle of the Somme, when suddenly all I could think of was Jamie Burrows – love-rat, coward and cheat.

Well, *he's* history now. Kirsty Baker is welcome to him.

It was Mum's idea to go to Scotland. She'd been there as a child and had magical memories of sparkly sea and long white beaches and oceans of purple heather. What's that they say about rose-tinted spectacles? So she rented a cottage in a place called Ardnamurchan, three kilometres along a stony track in the middle of nowhere. *An unspoilt, wilderness paradise*, the brochure said. It was a wilderness all right! There was nothing there but birds and it was six kilometres to the nearest shop. *Magnificent views of the Western Isles*, said the brochure.

We went for seven days. For the first six it rained unceasingly. Thick grey rain falling from even thicker grey banks of cloud. "So much for the magnificent views," said Alice, squinting through the cottage window.

Pete let the dice fall from the palm of his hand. "Six," he said, moving his silver battleship round the board.

"Coventry Street," I said. "My property – with a hotel – that's one thousand, one hundred and fifty pounds."

Pete was down to seventy-three pounds and the Old Kent Road. He threw his meagre pile of notes down on the table and said, "Bankrupt! I quit! Anyone fancy a cuppa?"

Mum was sitting on the window-seat sketching the wet garden.

"How many times are you going to paint the same soggy hedge?" Al said, with a yawn. She leaned back in her chair and stretched lazily.

"I'm waiting for the light to change," Mum said, dipping her paintbrush in a jar of water.

"There *isn't* any light!" said Al. "It's thick fog out there – we haven't seen the sun all week!"

"It's not fog in Scotland," shouted Pete from the kitchen. "It's mist. Scotch mist."

"It can't rain for ever," said Mum, biting the end of her brush.

I wasn't so sure.

"Your go, Al," I said. "You need to throw a double to get out of jail."

Al yawned. "Sorry, Iz," she said. "I've got Monopoly fatigue. You win. What's on TV?"

We started watching an old black-and-white movie about some island where all the whisky had run out. The actors had bad accents.

Pete came in with a tray of tea. "Has the ship run aground yet?" he said.

"What ship?" I said.

3

"The ship carrying all the whisky," said Pete. "It gets wrecked and the islanders steal the whisky and hide it in the caves."

"Thanks for giving the plot away, Pete," Al said, dunking a digestive biscuit into her tea.

"It was based on a true story," Pete said. "There was a book—"

"Great," I said, pulling a face at Al.

Suddenly Mum squealed. "Blue!" she said. "Look! Blue sky!"

"Quick," said Alice. "Let's escape. Before it starts raining again. Come on, Izzy."

It wasn't far to the beach. We walked along a sandy track across tufty grass and over some dunes. There were rabbits everywhere. The sky was brightening with every stride we took. The grey bits seemed to be parting like heavy curtains being pulled out of the way – like stage curtains opening to reveal a glittering set. All of a sudden we were on the top of a towering dune and below us was a steep wall of sand like a ski slope. "Run!" shouted Al, and grabbing my hand she hurtled towards the sea. She flung off her shoes and rolled up the legs of her jeans to her knees. Then she waded quickly into the water. "Come on Isabel, it's lovely!" she said.

I pulled off one trainer and dipped my toe in the edge of the wave. It was totally freezing. "Lying cow!" I said, splashing Alice with water.

The beach seemed to go on for ever. This was Mum's long white beach and there was her sparkly sea. We walked along the edge of the water where the waves left a lacy trail of shells. The sky had cleared completely and the sea was a deep blue. Out on the horizon were dozens of islands. They looked as though someone had flown over in a plane and scattered them there, like beads.

"Where did they come from?" I said, astonished.

"That's the *'magnificent view of the Western Isles'*," Al said. She sat down on the sugar-white sand and lit a cigarette.

"I thought you'd given up," I said.

"I had. But six days in a cottage with Mum and Pete and wall-to-wall Monopoly . . . God, Isabel, I've got the shakes. Look!" She held out her hand and twitched it manically.

"Daft cow," I said.

"That's twice you've called me a cow. Watch it or I'll drink these myself." Alice pulled two Bacardi Breezers out of her bag.

"Nice Alice," I said, patting her mop of fair hair. "Not a cow at all. Kind big sister."

"I even remembered a bottle-opener," she said with a grin.

The Bacardi Breezer was cold and lemony. I took a long swig and swallowed with a gulp. I was staring out to sea, gazing at the chain of islands, trailing my hand in the soft sand.

"Cheer up, Izzy – it might never happen," Al said. I smiled half-heartedly. I was thinking about Jamie Burrows. Alice can read me like a book. "You're not still thinking about Ego-boy, are you?" she said, pushing her hair decisively behind her ears.

I didn't answer.

"Forget him!" she said. "He's a jerk! He doesn't deserve you."

"Plenty of other fish in the sea," I said in a sarcastic voice.

"Damn right!" Al said. "Look at them all!" she pointed at the lapping waves. "The sea is heaving with them. Gorgeous men – kind, sensitive, loaded, fit!"

"As if!" I said, picking up a handful of sand. "All the nice-looking guys think they're God, and all the ugly guys are, well . . . ugly!"

"What about all the inbetweenie ones who look a bit dull but have wicked personalities and loads of hidden charm?" Al said.

"I don't know any of them," I said, letting the sand trickle through my fingers.

"I know dozens," Al said. "But most of them are gay!" She drank the last of her Bacardi and stuck the bottle in the sand. "Last cig," she said, opening her cigarette packet. She did a silly Scottish accent that made me laugh: "We'll need an expedition to the wee shop to restock supplies." Then she started tearing her cigarette packet open and rummaging in her bag.

"What are you doing?" I said.

"Looking for a pen," Al said.

"Why?" I asked.

"To write a message to all the lovely fish in the sea!"

Alice pulled out a biro and scribbled on the torn cardboard to get it going.

Then she wrote:

If there are any half-decent blokes out there who aren't axe murderers, egomaniacs or Britney Spears fans please contact Isabel Bright, 32 West Clarendon Street, Chorlton-cum-Hardy, Manchester M21 0RW.

"Now what?" I said, laughing.

Al tapped the side of her nose secretively. Then she rolled the message into a tight scroll and slid it into her empty Bacardi Breezer bottle. She took a stone and knocked the lid back in place. Then she handed the bottle back to me. "*You* can post it," she said.

"Post it?" I said, looking round the deserted beach.

"In the sea, dummy!" Al said. "Like castaways do."

We walked to the water's edge. A breeze was blowing across the sand, lifting the top off the waves in a fine spray. I took off my shoes and, braving the cold, I paddled out until the water was over my ankles. Gently, I lowered the message-in-a-bottle into the icy water. It bobbed and danced in front of me. Then the wind caught it and carried it out of reach. We watched it until it was out of view. By then my feet were numb with cold. Al handed me my shoes.

"I'm starving," she said, and turning her back on the sea, she started jogging across the sand.

Act I Scene i

Curtain rises. Two girls – one blonde, one dark – sit, backs to the wall, in a school corridor. One studies the pages of a book.

ISABEL:

Auditions for *The Tempest* were in the first week of term. Members of the Lower Sixth doing the Performing Arts A Level course – that's me – got to audition first. We were in the corridor outside the drama studio, in the Expressive Arts block. I was with Macy. We were running through lines.

"Have you got your lucky knickers on, honey?" she said.

"I wish," I said. "I'm nervous."

"You're supposed to be nervous – it's called ad-ren-a-lin, babe!" Macy said.

Macy's my best mate. She's American. She comes from Vermont.

"You be Prospero," I said. "I'll try it again." I started the opening speech:

"If by your art, my dearest father, you have put the wild waters in this roar, allay them . . ." I stopped. *"All*-ay them? All-*ay* them? . . . Which do you think is right?"

"The second one," Macy said, confidently.

"Sure?" I said.

"Sure," said Macy.

"Final answer?"

"Final answer."

". . . in this roar, all*ay* them."

"Brilliant!"

I was auditioning to be Miranda. As far as I could see, she appeared to be the only girl in the play. All the other characters were blokes or monsters – but that's Shakespeare for you. Our Performing Arts group has twelve girls and four boys. It's a casting director's nightmare! I'd been running through lines all weekend – I didn't want to be one of the ones in a stuck-on beard!

I continued: *"The sky, it seems, would pour down stinking pitch, but that the sea, mounting to th' welkin's cheek . . ."* I stopped again. "What's a welkin?" I asked.

Macy shrugged. "Search me!" she said.

I flipped to the back of the book and leafed through the notes.

"It means *sky*," I said, reading: *"the welkin's cheek – sky or heavens."*

"Why couldn't he just *say* sky?" Macy said, rolling her eyes.

"It wouldn't be Shakespeare, would it?" I said.

The door of the drama studio swung open. Kirsty Baker emerged, clutching a script. I looked away.

"I bet she was rubbish," said Macy, under her breath.

"Next, please!" said a voice from inside.

Inside the studio were two chairs. Ms Redman was sitting cross-legged on the floor in bare feet with piles of paper strewn in front of her. She's new. Our old drama teacher, Reggie Clarke, retired in the summer. We had a party for him and filled his briefcase with shaving foam.

"Isabel, isn't it?" Ms Redman said, ticking a list.

"Yes," I said.

"I'd like you to read for Miranda," she said. "Sebastian will read Prospero, to give you someone to bounce off."

Sebastian Reeves was leaning against the wall reading a script and muttering under his breath. I pictured myself bouncing off him – as if he was a inflatable castle or something – and had to suppress a fit of the giggles. Sebastian's a bit on the big side. He's a brilliant actor though. He's got this amazing booming voice. The fact that he would be playing Prospero was a dead cert. He's the best in the group by miles. (Sebastian's got an uncle who's a famous actor called Jason something-or-other – he's on the telly a lot – plays rogueish types with red faces and Cockney accents in Victorian costume dramas.)

Ms Redman was looking at me. "I'd like you to do the speech from Act I Scene ii," she said. "Miranda's just witnessed the storm and the wrecking of the ship. She's distressed, and she suspects that her father, Prospero, has somehow caused the violent weather."

I cleared my throat and did deep diaphragm breathing. *Distressed*, I told myself, *think distressed*.

"Use the chairs if you want to," she said.

Sebastian strode over and sat down decisively on one of the chairs. I looked at the black wall of the studio and tried to imagine raging sea and crashing waves. I thought of Ardnamurchan.

"Start when you're ready," Ms Redman said.

I glanced at Sebastian. His bushy eyebrows were twitching.

Not wanting to laugh or be distracted, I stared hard at his knees and started my speech: "*If by your art, my dearest father, you have put the wild waters in this roar . . .*"

When I said, "*O! I have suffered with those that I saw suffer!*", I took a step away from Sebastian and put my hand on my chest. It was a bit of a hammy gesture. I regretted it instantly.

On "*Had I been any god of power . . .*" I waved my arms in the air as if I was frustrated. I'd tried that in the mirror at home and it looked OK there – but here, with the script in my hand, it felt awkward.

Sebastian rose from his chair and said, in his fruity voice, "*Be collected. No more amazement. Tell your piteous heart there's no harm done.*" He laid his hand on my shoulder.

"*O, woe the day!*" I said. I tried to sound really upset. I wasn't sure if it worked or if it sounded cheesy. Ms Redman was writing something on a piece of paper. Was she writing "deeply moving" or was she writing "deeply corny"?

Sebastian started a great long speech which he did without the book. Show off! I was so thrown that I lost my place in the script and missed the cue for my next line. There was an embarrassing silence and then Ms Redman said, "Miranda?"

My face flushed red as I said, hurriedly: "*More to know did never muddle with my thoughts.*"

Then Sebastian was off again. When he said: "*Lend thy hand and pluck my magic garment from me,*" he gestured to me and I mimed taking a cloak off his shoulders. I tried to do it convincingly – and I think it worked. "Attention to detail is the key to mime," Mr Clarke used to say.

Ms Redman wrote something on her sheet. Sebastian was in the middle of a sentence when she waved her hand to stop us. "Lovely," she said. "That was very good. You move very well, Isabel."

I smiled. "Thank you," I said.

* * *

Outside, Macy was looking at me expectantly.

"Well?" she said. "Did you wow her?"

"She said I move very well," I said, shaking my hips.

"But did you get the part?" Macy said.

"Thursday," I said. "She said she'll tell us by Thursday."

Act I Scene ii

Enter Macy and Isabel. Isabel is eating olives from a Tupperware pot.

ISABEL:

I got the part of Miranda. I was *so* pleased.

Macy got the part of Ariel. "He's a spirit," she said.

"The spirit of clean washing," I said. "Ariel washes whiter!"

Macy ignored the joke. "When I saw it in New York, Ariel flew in on a wire," she said, "and he was wearing this silver Lycra all-in-one number, like a bobsleigh rider."

"Groovy!" I said.

"The best bit is I get to sing," Macy said. Macy's got a great voice – it's kind of like Dido meets Missy Elliot.

We were reading the noticeboard outside the drama studio. I was hopping up and down with delight.

"Prospero – Sebastian Reeves," said Macy. "There's a surprise! Miranda – Isabel Bright, Ariel – Macy Paige, blah blah blah . . . Iris – Kirsty Baker."

"Who's Iris?" I said.

"She's some sort of goddess," Macy said. "But don't worry, she's only in one scene – it's a crap part!"

"Ferdinand – Jamie Burrows," I said, running my finger down the list. "Who's Ferdinand?"

"Uh-oh," said Macy, pulling a face.

"What?" I said.

"Ferdinand is Miranda's lover," she said.

"Oh great!" I said, sarcastically. I had a sudden sinking feeling in my stomach.

Pete had cooked a chilli. It was one of his hotter ones – the sort that makes your eyes smart and your nose run. I filled my glass a second time. Then I said, "I'm Miranda."

No one was listening.

"I'm Miranda," I said again. "in *The Tempest*."

"Miranda?" said Mum. "Which one's she?" She was fanning her mouth. "Pass me the water please, Alice," she said.

"The *main* part!" I said, expecting a better reaction.

"I thought Prospero was the main part," Al said, tearing a piece of pitta bread in half.

"Well," I said, "the second biggest part." Since when was *she* an expert on Shakespeare? She's a Maths student!

"Great," said Mum. "Well done, love." She was more bothered about her burning lips. "Heavens, Pete! How many chillies did you put in this?" She opened her mouth wide and gulped in air.

"That's great, Iz!" Al said. She flashed me a big grin. "Clever little sis. Just don't forget to thank us when you make your Oscar speech." She clutched the pepper grinder like an Oscar statuette and said: ". . . and not forgetting my stepfather, Pete, who made me chilli, and my sister, Al, who taught me everything I know . . ." We laughed.

Pete was obliviously scooping up huge forkfuls of chilli. He must have a flameproof mouth.

"What does Miranda get up to then?" he asked.

"Well," I said. "She lives on an island with her dad, and she falls in love with someone called Ferdinand—"

"Played by?" Alice interrupted. She looked at me with her eyebrows raised.

"Jamie Burrows," I said flatly.

"Ah!" said Mum.

They all stopped eating and looked at me sympathetically.

"That's unfortunate," Mum said.

Unfortunate? I could think of better words!

"Will you have to kiss him?" Al said, taking a chunk of tomato out of the salad bowl.

"I don't know," I said dismissively. "I haven't read the whole play yet!" All three of them were staring at me as if I had a sudden terrible illness and wasn't going to make it to the end of the meal. "It's not *that* big a deal," I said. "I'll just be professional about it. It's a *play*! I only have to *pretend* to like him."

Pete brandished a ladle. "Anyone for more chilli?" he said.

We all politely refused.

Mum was piling salad on to her plate. "I don't know *The Tempest*," she said. "What's it about?"

What *is* it about? I haven't really worked that out yet.

"Islands," I said, vaguely. "Islands and storms . . . and shipwrecks . . ."

"Does it have a happy ending?" said Pete, wiping bread round his plate.

"I don't know," I said. "I'll let you know."

Act I Scene iii

Lights up on sixteen people in a room with black walls and no windows.

ISABEL:

The first read-through was on Friday. Ms Redman had put the chairs in a big circle in the drama studio. She gave us all a script and put a pot of pencils on the floor in the middle of the circle. "You all need a pencil – to mark cuts in the text. Help yourself if you haven't got one."

I fished in my bag and unzipped my pencil case. Across the circle, Jamie Burrows got up and walked to the pencil pot. I noticed he was wearing the Purple Ronnie socks I bought him for Valentine's Day. Kirsty Baker was sitting beside him in a pair of skintight jeans. She was smiling smugly, like a fisherman with a twenty-pound salmon.

Ms Redman started speaking. "Let's make a start then," she said. She was wearing earrings with blue glass beads that twinkled when she shook her head. "Before we read the play – just a few details about the production and the way we'll be working. As you know, I'm new to you, but I've heard great things about you all from Mr Clarke . . ."

Good old Reggie. He said we were his favourite group in thirty-five years of teaching. Bless!

". . . so I'm sure it's going to be a great show. It's an ambitious play to do and the rehearsal period is tight. Performances will be on October seventeenth, eighteenth and nineteenth, just before half term, so we've just under six weeks to put it all together. The sheet I'm giving you gives performance dates and outlines the rehearsal schedule." She handed a pile of pink sheets to Sara Bottomley. "Take one and pass them on," she said.

Macy handed me a sheet.

"Some of the rehearsals will be in your Performing Arts lessons but we'll also be rehearsing after school and you'll see there are two Saturday rehearsals planned."

"Miss, I've got a job on Saturdays," said Natalie Roberts.

"Well, you'll have to make other arrangements," Ms Redman said. "One of the conditions of doing this course is availability for rehearsals and performances outside school hours. That was spelt out clearly in the Sixth Form Handbook."

Natalie Roberts pulled a face and mouthed "As if!" to Chloe Stretton.

"Theatre's about teamwork," Ms Redman said. She folded her bare feet under her on the chair and flicked her hair out of her eyes. "If one person falls down, the whole play falls down. We work together – everyone giving one hundred per cent – or preferably one hundred-and-ten per cent."

Behind Ms Redman's back Andy Shaw did a Hitler salute. Macy smirked.

"Sebastian may have the biggest role," Ms Redman continued, "but you're all equally important. There are no stars – this isn't Hollywood, it's theatre."

The read-through was a slog. It took hours. Thank God for Sebastian Reeves! At least he could say his lines without stumbling over the words – which is more than most of the cast could. I did my lines OK although I didn't seem to have many of them, now it came to it.

Macy was great. She even sang. "What's the tune?" she said, when it came to: *Full fathom five thy father lies* . . . "Shall I just improvise?" Ms Redman looked impressed.

When Jamie Burrows was doing Ferdinand's lines to Miranda he kept looking across the circle at me, trying to catch my eye. I ignored him and stared at my script. Daft ponce! At the end, when we were stacking the chairs, he came up behind me and said, "You were great, Isabel."

"What did you expect?" I said coolly. I caught a whiff of his body spray. Obsession by Calvin Klein. How appropriate!

* * *

It was nearly dark by the time we left school. I called Mum to tell her we were going to La Viva for cream cheese bagels. Macy had a singing lesson at seven and she didn't have time to get home for dinner and then back.

We sat at our favourite table by the window.

"Well," said Macy. "Wasn't *that* thrilling?"

The waitress brought us two large of cappuccinos. Macy dipped her finger in the froth.

"First readings are always dire," I said. "It will be fine."

"What do you think of Ms Redman?" Macy said, licking her finger.

"I like her," I said. "I like her no-shit approach. Tough but tender! And I like her hair." Ms Redman's hair is thick and black and cut in a bob that swings around her shoulders.

"L'Oreal!" said Macy, tossing her hair, "because she's worth it!"

I laughed.

"She's got a big nose, though," Macy said.

"Nothing wrong with big noses," I said. I've got a big nose. Lower down the school I used to get called Miss Piggy.

My bagel arrived. The cream cheese was melting down the side. I dipped my knife in a pool of it. Just then my phone beeped at me.

"Text message, honey," Macy said, biting into her bacon roll.

I pulled out my phone. There was a message from Jamie Burrows. It said: *"Dear Miranda Thought U looked great tonite! Luv Ferdinand"*.

I showed it to Macy. She snorted with disgust. "Like you give a shit!" she said, handing my phone back to me. She sipped her cappuccino and it left a tidemark of foam on her top lip. "How cheesy is *that*?" she said, wiping her mouth with a napkin.

"Reply?" my phone asked me.

"Erase," I pressed. "Not likely," I said.

Act I Scene iv

Enter Isabel in a leotard and tights. She ties back her hair in a velvet scrunchy.

ISABEL:

Saturday morning is my favourite time of the week. I get to lie-in till eight o'clock instead of getting up at quarter to seven, like on school days. Then Mum runs me to dancing. I do ballet from nine until ten, and jazz dance from ten until eleven. Then I catch a bus to my singing lesson at eleven-thirty. Pete collects me at twelve-thirty and I go home and have a hot bath. Bliss! I love dancing and I love singing. When I'm a famous actress, every day will be like Saturday and I'll be in that *My Kind of Day* slot at the back of the Radio Times . . . Dream on, Isabel!

My dance teacher – who's called Siobhan – has long gristly legs and the most manky feet you ever saw. They're all bumps and knobbles and horny skin. "All dancers have horrible feet," she says, "no gain without pain. Agony and ecstasy are two sides of the same coin." That's why I want to be an actor not a dancer. I'll go for the ecstasy without the agony, thanks.

"I got the part of Miranda," I said. We were taking a break between ballet and jazz. Siobhan was swigging a bottle of Evian.

"Congratulations!" she said.

I sat on the floor, legs astride and stretched over, resting my chin on my knee. "We've got this new drama teacher," I said. "She's called Ms Redman. She's a bit—" I was going to say "strict" but Siobhan interrupted me.

"Doe Redman?" she said.

"Doe?" I said. What kind of name was that?

"Small, dark hair, big nose?" Siobhan said.

I nodded.

"I know her," Siobhan said, lifting her heel on to the bar.

"What's she like?" I said.

"She'll make you work hard," Siobhan said. "Not like Reggie Clarke and his easy-does-it approach!"

"She says I move well," I said, sitting up and peeling a banana.

"So I should think," Siobhan said, winking at me. "You've been well taught."

There was no one at the bus stop but me, so I practised my lines. I'd just about got my head round Act I Scene ii – the one we'd done at the audition.

"O, I have suffered with those that I saw suffer! A brave

vessel, who had, no doubt, some noble creature in her, dashed all to pieces."

I couldn't remember what was after that, so I fished in my bag for the script, but then the bus came.

The journey to my singing lesson goes right by Jamie Burrows' house. Since we split up I make a point of not looking at the house as we go by. It's right opposite the traffic lights, two doors down from the Chinese takeaway. The lights were red.

"O, I have suffered," I whispered under my breath. Too right I've suffered. *"O, the cry did knock against my very heart."* We were right outside his window. I was on the top deck of the bus. If I looked to the right I would be looking into Jamie's bedroom. Jamie's bedroom – scene of many hours of ecstasy – with its Manchester United duvet cover and Britney Spears calendar.

I couldn't stop myself. I glanced right. The curtains were drawn like at the end of a play. *Curtain falls on Isabel and Jamie.* The bus engine throbbed. Then, just as it lurched forward, the curtain drew to one side and I saw Jamie's face, foggy with sleep, and his hair, ungelled and sticking up like hedgehog bread. I looked away quickly.

"O woe the day!" I said, glancing back at my script.

Mr O'Leary had a cold. His nose was shiny and red.

"We'll start with scales," he said, and he played middle C on the piano.

I sang up the scale.

"Lift the soft pallette. Space in the mouth. Nice open aah sound," he said, blowing his nose on a big spotty handkerchief.

I sang another scale.

"Now sing me your breakfast," he said. He always does that. He gives me a note and I have to sing whatever I had for breakfast, all on one note.

"O-range j-ooce and mue-sli with yog-urt on top," I sang.

"Ve-ry health-y," he sang back, his voice croaking a little because of his cold. "Now," he said. "Again. Same words, but this time sing up the scale and let's have a delicious crescendo."

I took a deep breath.

"Breathe down to your feet," he said. "All the way to the carpet."

I breathed again, feeling my chest inflate like a set of bellows. And then I sang my breakfast menu, getting louder and louder until "yog-urt" boomed out.

"Good," he said. "Now stretch your face out!"

I waggled my face about as if I had a terrible itch and blew my cheeks out like balloons. When I first started coming here for lessons I used to feel a prat doing that, but now I don't care.

"OK," Mr O'Leary said, spinning round on the piano stool. "What have you practised?"

I sang a song by Mozart. It's not really the kind of thing I want to sing but Mr O'Leary says arias are good for producing a good clean voice. They make you sing through your head, he says. I sang it OK. OK-*ish*.

"Not bad," he said. "Let's try that last phrase again. Relax into the high note and just let it float out. Sing through your *eyes*, Isabel."

I tried again, focusing my eyes on the curtain rail and pressing the soles of my feet into the carpet, the way he's told me. This time the top note seemed to come out of me by itself. It sounded wonderful. Sometimes, when I get it right, it feels as if I'm flying – riding on air currents like a bird.

"Beautiful," he said, beaming at me from his red-rimmed eyes. "Very beautiful."

Pete was in the car. He was eating a bag of Minstrels. "Do you want one?" he said.

"No thanks," I said. I wanted to be thin to play Miranda. Thin and spot-free.

I went straight upstairs to run a bath when we got back. I poured coconut bath foam under the hot tap. My legs were aching from dance. I bent over to stretch out my calf muscles, pointing my toe on the edge of the bath.

Mum came into the bathroom. "You got a letter," she said. "It's on your bed."

"Who's it from?" I said.

"Someone in Scotland," Mum said. "It's got a Western Isles postmark."

"Scotland?" I said. "I don't know anyone in Scotland! Will you fetch it for me?"

"What did your last slave die of?" Mum said. But she brought it anyway.

"Cheers, Mum! You're a star," I said, lowering myself into the hot bubbles. I looked at the envelope. The handwriting was small and sloping: Isabel Bright, 32 West Clarendon Street . . . I ripped it open. The bathroom was full of steam. *"Dear Isabel,"* it said, *"I'm definitely not an axe murderer. I hope I'm not an egomaniac, and as for Britney – I think she's pants . . ."*

Act I Scene v

Early morning. A tall young man walks along the shore with a hairy black dog.

DUNCAN:

I've found many things on this shore – plastic oil drums and shoes and fishermen's floats and enough planks of wood to build a house – but I never thought I'd find a message in a bottle. Not a real one, from a real person. The tide was on its way back out. There was a thick slimy belt of seaweed hugging the bay at the high water mark, and tangled into it were shells and bits of rope and a few dead seagulls. The bottle caught my eye. I don't know why. There were plenty of other bottles on the beach. Perhaps I was meant to find it.

It was half-buried in sand. I picked it up and brushed it clean. The label had washed off. Something was stuffed inside it – rolled tightly and wedged into the neck of the bottle. Paper or cardboard, perhaps. I prised off the lid with a stone and slid out a Silk Cut packet, soaking wet and turning to mush. I unrolled it carefully so that it wouldn't tear. There was writing on the back of it and, though the ink had smudged, I could just make out what it said – and the name. "Isabel Bright," I said aloud to myself. "Isabel Bright from Manchester." I slipped the message back inside the bottle, put the bottle into my coat pocket and walked across the dunes to the road. Immediately my head filled with messages, sentences, opening lines . . .

When I got back, the house was empty. I made a pile of toast and jam. Then I sat at the kitchen table with my feet on the stove and wrote a letter. This is what I wrote:

Dear Isabel

I'm definitely not an axe murderer. I hope I'm not an egomaniac, and as for Britney – I think she's pants. Whether or not I'm half-decent . . . well that's a hard one to judge. I could put you in touch with my best friend Ned who'd say that I'm mad and crap at pool, or with my mum who'd say I'm untidy but affectionate. And my music teacher would say I'm a genius. But half-decent? Judge for yourself.

My name is Duncan MacLeod (pronounced Muck-Cloud) and I live on the Isle of Rimsay which is in the Outer Hebrides – which is off the west coast of Scotland in case you're no good at geography. I'm in the Upper Sixth doing A Levels in English, Maths and Music. I'm lead singer and rhythm guitarist in a band called the Posh

Porpoises. I also play five-a-side football (we haven't got enough players for eleven-a-side) and table tennis. I like movies, Yorkie Bars and McFlurry ice creams (the Crunchie ones) – although the nearest McDonalds is a six-hour ferry trip away!

Please write back. I'm dying to know what drove you to send desperate SOS messages. And how exactly *did* your message in a bottle get to me from Manchester when Manchester isn't by the sea? Tell all.

Yours decently and curiously,
Duncan MacLeod

Act I Scene vi

Enter Macy, in a yellow bath robe.

MACY:

Imagine getting a letter out of the blue from a guy you've never met, who's actually found your message in a bottle! How romantic is that?

Isabel was pretty cool about it. "You never told me you'd sent a message in a bottle," I said. She was lying on my bed. It was Saturday afternoon.

"It was a joke!" she said. "I didn't even write it. Al did. We never expected anyone to *find* it!"

"So it's a miracle!" I said. "It's magic. It's one of life's mysteries. You write a letter – he finds it! It's the stuff of fairy tales. The stuff of dreams!"

"It's just a coincidence," Isabel said with a shrug.

Coincidence? Is she kidding? Has this girl got no soul? If it was me that had gotten the letter I'd be telling everyone I know. I'd have kissed the postman! I'd be telling the local paper and appearing on TV. I'd write a novel about it. A movie screenplay perhaps. At the very least, I'd be a *little* excited.

"He's written you a letter!" I said, throwing a

cushion at her. "A letter! Not only does he find and read your message – *six weeks* after you wrote it – he writes a letter back the very same day. He must be one nice guy, Izzy!"

"He might just be bored!" Isabel said. "I don't suppose there's much to do on the Isle of wherever it is!"

The letter was lying on my bedroom floor. I picked it up. "May I?" I said.

"Be my guest," Isabel said. She took my Dido CD out of its case and slid it into the CD player.

"He sounds great," I said. "He's funny, he's musical, he's affectionate, he plays football, he likes ice cream . . . What more do you want?" I unwrapped the towel and rubbed my wet hair.

"I want you to cut the Mills and Boon match-made-in-heaven stuff," said Isabel. "Just because some sad guy stranded on a Scottish island wants to be my pen-pal, I don't have to fall in love with him!"

The trouble with Isabel is . . . well, how can I put it? The trouble with Isabel is Jamie Burrows. She needs to move on – get him out of her system. It's like he snipped her heart into lots of pieces and threw them in the garbage and she's still trying to reassemble the bits.

"*Yours decently and curiously, Duncan MacLeod*," I said. "Sweet!"

Isabel was singing along with Dido.

"Duncan," I said, over the music. "Not the most sexy of names is it? Dunkin Donuts!"

"What?" said Isabel, laughing.

"Dunkin Donuts," I said. "It's a fast-food chain that started over in the States. You get a box of donuts and a little pot of chocolate sauce and you dunk the donuts in the sauce."

"Dunkin Donuts," said Isabel, with a snort of laughter. "Dunkin Duncan!"

Act I Scene vii

Enter Isabel, barefoot, script in hand.

ISABEL:

My first rehearsal was on Tuesday. We blocked the whole of Act I Scene ii – my first scene – who's on stage when, who stands where, who enters or exits from which side. It's such a long scene. It goes on for twenty pages. It took us two hours just to walk through all the moves!

First there's the bit with me and Prospero – the bit I read at the audition – where we're talking about the storm and the wrecked ship: *"O I have suffered . . ."* etc. Then Prospero tells me all this stuff about how we come to be on the island: how we arrived twelve years ago (when I was three) in another shipwreck, after his brother (my uncle Antonio) had overthrown him as Duke of Milan and dumped us onboard a leaky ship. Then I ask Prospero why he caused the storm we've just witnessed: *"I pray you, Sir, for still 'tis beating in my mind, your reason for raising this sea-storm?"* Prospero ducks the question but explains that the storm has (surprise surprise!) washed ashore his old enemies – my uncle Antonio and his partner in crime the King of Naples. They – and others – are now, apparently, on our island. After this, Miranda falls asleep – presumably exhausted by all this news!

While I'm asleep, Ariel (Macy) – Prospero's elfish servant – comes on stage. Prospero tells Ariel to make himself invisible so that he can do more magic. Then I wake up and go with Prospero to visit Caliban (Andy Shaw) – a foul monster who lives in a cave and works as Prospero's slave. Caliban and Prospero have an argument and I make a speech about how horrible Caliban is. Then Prospero sends him off to collect firewood and Ariel (who is now invisible – tricky one for Macy!) sings a song about yellow sands and wild sea (sounds like our beach at Ardnamurchan!). At this point Ferdinand, the shipwrecked son of the King of Naples (Jamie Burrows – everybody say *BOO!*) appears, drawn by the magical song. Miranda and Ferdinand meet and fall in love in about three seconds. Then Prospero decides to give Ferdinand a hard time to make sure he's worthy of Miranda. He tells him he'll have to eat acorns and drink seawater. Nice one, Prospero! And off they all go. And that's just *one* scene . . .

Ms Redman had asked Jamie to come at five o'clock. We were doing the bit with Caliban when he arrived. He'd been home and changed out of his school uniform. He had his denim jacket on. The one from Hennes. The one I helped him choose. I really like it. I used to borrow it sometimes. Used to.

I looked at Sebastian Reeves, who was wearing a baggy purple sweatshirt.

"*Come forth I say*," he shouted at Andy Shaw.

"Am I going to have an actual cave, Miss?" said Andy Shaw.

"You'll be concealed under a blanket," Ms Redman said. She walked to centre stage. "About here. When Prospero calls you, I want you to roll out from under the cover in a reptilian sort of way."

Reptilian. That wouldn't be difficult. Andy Shaw is the ugliest guy I know.

Ms Redman threw Andy a piece of old curtain from the props cupboard. "Use this for now," she said. Andy wrapped it round his head like a shawl.

"You look like the Virgin Mary," Macy said.

Ms Redman laughed. "Carry on," she said.

Sebastian started doing the bit where he insults Caliban: "*Thou poisonous slave . . . filth as thou art . . .*"

"Miss, why are they all so horrible to me?" Andy Shaw said.

"Well," said Ms Redman, "for starters, you tried to rape Miranda—"

"Gross!" said Macy. She was sitting cross-legged on the stage, circling her head around her shoulders, like we do in rehearsal warm-ups.

"We'll come back to all the whys and wherefores when you're more familiar with the text," Ms Redman said. "Let's get the blocking done for this section so we can get on to Ferdinand's bit." Jamie waved and flashed her his best smile. Greaseball!

We walked through the next page until Sebastian said, *"So slave, hence!"* and Caliban exited stage right. Then Macy started singing. Jamie had to hear the music and gradually walk towards it, as if he was bewitched.

"You'll be at the back," Ms Redman said. "And you'll come down the aisle through the audience, drawn by the magical singing."

"Very magical," I said, winking at Macy.

"Miranda, you'll be down stage right when Ferdinand first sees you. You haven't seen him yet, so stay with your back to him until line four-hundred and ten."

I scribbled her directions on to my script.

"Now turn," she said.

I turned and, looking at Ferdinand, I said: *"What is't? A spirit?"*

Ms Redman explained that Miranda thinks Ferdinand is some sort of ghost but Prospero tells her he's real and she says, *"I might call him a thing divine . . ."*

"I might call him plenty of things," said Macy, behind me, just loud enough for me to hear. I glanced at her and smirked. "Divine's not the first word that comes to mind," she muttered.

Jamie Burrows was getting nearer and nearer. His hair gel glistened in the studio lights. He was doing his self-pity bit about seeing his father drown. I have to sound all sympathetic and say, *"Alack for mercy."* Ms Redman wanted me to take hold of his hands and gaze lovingly at him on this line. That was some challenge to my acting ability. I'd rather have slapped his silly face! I took hold of his hands and stared him out. Then he has what must be the cheesiest line in the whole play. He says, basically, if you're a virgin and you're not any one else's bird you can marry me and be Queen of Naples. As if he'd get away with a line like that! Up yours, Ferdinand, would be my response! But Miranda just looks adoringly at him. Dream on Shakespeare! What planet were you on?

We went to La Viva after the rehearsal for a quick coffee. And a chocolate muffin.

"Dickhead!" said Macy.

"Who – Ferdinand or Jamie Burrows?" I said.

"Both," said Macy. "And Shakespeare! It's all so sexist! There's Miranda stuck on a desert island and what's the choice Shakespeare gives her? Caliban or Ferdinand? She only falls for Ferdinand because she's desperate. The girl's fifteen and the only men she's ever seen are a horny reptilian monster and her dad!"

I pulled the cellophane off my double choc chip muffin and broke it in half. "What do you think Doe stands for?" I said.

"Doe?" said Macy.

"That's what she's called," I said, "Ms Redman. She's called Doe. Doe Redman. That's what Siobhan says."

"Doe?" said Macy, biting into the muffin. "I dunno . . . Doris? Dorothy?"

"Dolores?" I suggested. "Or Di-do?"

"Dil-do?" said Macy with a grin. "Or Do-nut!"

I knew what was coming next.

"Have you written back to Dunkin Donuts yet?" Macy said.

How did I know she'd ask? She's gone on and on about my *mystery* letter. My *miracle* letter. My romantic voice from the blue. Macy's watched too many movies. That's her trouble.

"No," I said, sucking on a chocolate chip.

"Are you going to?" she said.

"Maybe," I said.

I wish I'd never let Alice write the stupid message. I mean, what sort of impression does it give? Get in touch with Isabel Bright. She's desperate! She'll have anyone! It's as bad as placing a small ad in the lonely hearts column: *Sad girl, 16, WLTM guy with two legs – GSOH – for fun and letter-writing.*

"He might be gorgeous," Macy said, licking chocolate off her lips. "Ask him to send a photo."

What is this, a dating agency?

"Macy," I said. "I'm seriously *not* interested. So drop it."

Act I Scene viii

Enter Isabel in leggings and a crop top. She is stretching in front of the mirror.

ISABEL:

Like I said to Macy, I'm totally not interested in Duncan what's-his-face. He's probably seven feet tall with bushy red hair and a kilt. But it did seem a bit tight not to write back to him so I wrote a letter:

Dear Duncan

Thanks for your letter. Wow! What a coincidence, you finding my bottle on your island. It hadn't come from Manchester – only Ardnamurchan, but still . . . I hope you didn't get the wrong impression from the message. It wasn't serious. My sister wrote it. We were just mucking about on holiday. Actually, it was meant to be a letter to the fish – not that they can read, or anything!

So, what can I tell you? My name – well you know that already. Actually I used to be called Isabel Brownlow, but then my mum got married again to Pete Bright so now I'm Isabel Bright – which is a bit of a daft name. Pete's favourite joke is: *Is-a-bell bright? It depends if you polish it or not*! Corny isn't it? At school when I was younger, some of the teachers used to call me Little Miss Bright, which was pretty nauseating. I think when I'm an actress I'll go back to Isabel Brownlow. My family call me Izzy or Iz – or sometimes Busy-Izzy. But that's quite enough about my name.

I love acting and dancing and singing and parties and shoes and Dido and olives. I hate mud and Britney and mindless violence and McDonalds (six hours to the nearest McDisgustings would suit me fine!). I'm also in the Sixth Form – in the Lower Sixth – doing Performing Arts, English, French and Textiles. Performing Arts is my best subject. We've just started rehearsals for *The Tempest* in which I play a character called Miranda who is a bit of a drip. My best friend Macy is in the play too. Macy is a mad American – five foot nothing with a big bum and and a loud voice. She wants to be a stand-up comedian, or a pop icon – think Bjork meets Ruby Wax and you'll get the picture.

I live with my mum (who's a nurse) and my stepdad Pete (who runs a company called Bright Computers) and my big sister Alice – except that she's away most of the time at university in Edinburgh. And we've got a black cat called Cleopatra who drags herself across the carpet on

her belly like a commando if you tell her to swim.
Smart cat!

So that's me.

I hope that satisfies your curiosity!

Yours undesperately

Isabel

I hadn't meant to write that much, but what the heck!
I posted it anyway.

"Does it need a special stamp to go all that way?"
I asked the woman in the post office. She checked on
her chart.

"No, it's still British Isles, love," she said.
"Nineteen pence."

"It's free if you put it in a bottle," I said. She looked
at me like I was weird.

Act II Scene i

Curtain opens on the kitchen at Isabel's house. Isabel is making a toasted sandwich with sundried tomatoes and mozzarella.

ISABEL:

What was it that I liked about Jamie Burrows? I often ask myself that. I didn't really know him until Year Ten when he auditioned for the summer musical. It was *West Side Story*. We had the lead parts. I was Maria and he was Tony – destined from the start to be stage lovers!

Jamie couldn't dance and there was this routine we had to do while we were singing: "*Tonight, tonight . . .*" In the movie they're on a fire escape, up and down ladders, high above New York. We had a few rostra blocks and the scaffolding tower that the technical crew use for fixing up the lights, so we had to work hard to get the same effect. Mr Clarke wasn't very hot on choreography so he asked me to sort out a routine. I worked on it with Siobhan a bit at my dancing lesson. Then I had to teach it to Jamie. We stayed behind on our own in the drama studio one night after school. We worked on it for ages. It all comes to a climax when he's singing: "*Maria, I just met a girl called Maria . . .*" and she's singing: "*Tonight, tonight, won't be just any night . . .*" We did a kind of tango across the stage and then I span around and swung up on to the scaffolding tower. From there I had to jump off the tower into his arms, and he had to catch me and kiss me.

That was when it happened. The first time we rehearsed the kiss. He kissed me as Tony, holding me up at chest height, like we'd planned. Then he lowered me to the floor and kissed me again, as Jamie. He kissed me for longer than he needed to. Deliciously long. And then the cleaner came banging in with her floor polisher.

"Oh my God!" she said. "You made me jump! I thought everyone had gone!"

Jamie asked me out the next day. We went out together for over a year – one year, one month and five days. We were a golden couple – Posh and Becks, only not so loaded, Richard and Judy, only not so cheesy, Romeo and Juliet, only not so complicated. We were even Cinderella and Prince Charming in the Christmas panto. How corny is that?

He was my first love. First proper boyfriend. First kiss. Don't they say the first cut is the deepest? I loved the way he looked at me, with the edges of his mouth turning up ever so slightly and his huge brown eyes fixed on mine – eyes you could drown in. He's a great kisser too. Not that I've got much to compare him with – only Sebastian Reeves in *Beauty and the Beast* (too much tongue) and Andy Shaw in a game of spin the bottle at Natalie Roberts' birthday party (too many cheese-and-onion crisps!).

Act III Scene i is the big love scene between Miranda and Ferdinand. Our first rehearsal was on Friday. I wasn't looking forward to it.

"Just be professional," Macy said, as we made our way to the drama studio. "Think of it as a role play. Miranda is something you put on – like a cloak. You become Miranda. Miranda loves Ferdinand. Then when you leave the rehearsal, you take the cloak off and you're Isabel again. Isabel who hates Jamie Burrows' guts."

I wish I hated him as much as Macy thinks I do.

Doe was there waiting for us. We didn't go straight into the scene. She made us do a warm-up, barefoot – lots of slow bending and stretching like Tai Chi. There were only four of us there – Doe and me and Jamie and Sebastian. I felt pretty self-conscious. Ms Redman made us lie on our backs on the floor and hum. Then she told us to choose a line from the scene we were about to rehearse and say it over and over to ourselves. After a few minutes of doing that we had to crawl on all fours around the room whispering our line to each other. I looked through the script and chose the line: *"My father is hard at study. Pray now, rest yourself."* It was a fairly neutral line – not too embarassing. Jamie's line was more direct: *"The very instant that I saw you did my heart fly to your service."* When we knew our line off by heart, and we'd finished crawling on our hands and knees, we had to take it in turns to stand up and say our line in lots of different ways – as if we were scared, as if we were angry, or drunk, or shy, or newly in love.

"Wrap the words in the emotion," Ms Redman said. ". . . OK, good, well done. Right, Sebastian take a break. Isabel and Jamie, I'd like you to do a quick improvisation to get you in the mood for the scene."

We had to improvise meeting for the first time in a nightclub.

"You're very attracted to each other," Doe said. "Love at first sight. So what do you say to each other?"

"Voulez-vous couchez avec moi, ce soir?" said Sebastian Reeves, watching from the side.

Jamie smirked. Then, straightening his face he looked into my eyes and said, "You have the most wonderful smile."

Pass the sick-bag! "Thanks," I said. "Can I get you a drink?" Independent woman, taking control. No simpering . . .

"You light up the room like the sun," he said.

When did you last hear someone use that chat up line down the Oxford Road?

"Shall we dance then?" I said. He took hold of my hands and started twirling me about. Despite all my coaching he still can't dance. I laughed with embarassment.

"OK, let's block the scene," said Doe. "From the top."

The scene starts with Ferdinand carrying heavy logs down the aisle and into centre stage – part of the harsh treatment Prospero is using to test him. Enter Miranda from stage right, full of pity for him, and Prospero – playing gooseberry, spying on them from a distance – standing on the rostra upstage left. Miranda (thinking her dad is hard at work with his magic books) tells Ferdinand to have a rest: *"My father is hard at study, pray now, rest yourself."* She volunteers to help him carry the logs so that he can chat to her and still get his work done on time. He says she couldn't possibly – she is a girl after all. Then he asks her her name and she says: *"Miranda."* We're both centre stage at this point, facing each other. Ferdinand, walking downstage left and addressing the audience, starts talking about how he's been about a bit and has admired lots of beautiful women but that she, Miranda (he turns to face me again), is perfect, peerless and best. Miranda (walking downstage right) says that her own face in the mirror is the only woman she's ever seen, so she doesn't know how she compares to the rest of womankind, and that she hasn't seen many blokes either but that he seems a nice enough boy. He tells her his heart is her slave and that though he's really a prince, he's lifting logs for her sake. They are both downstage now, but wide apart. Miranda (looking him in the eye) asks the million dollar question: *"Do you love me?"* And Ferdinand says he does. At this Miranda turns her back on him, sinks to her knees and starts crying. Ferdinand walks over to comfort her and asks, *"Wherefore weep you?"* (Wherefore indeed!) Miranda says it's because she isn't worthy of him. (How pathetic is that?) Ferdinand puts his hands on her shoulders. At which point she pulls herself together, stands up, turns round and says she'll be his wife, if he'll marry her. And he says yes, he'll be her husband, thank you very much. (Just like that.) *"Here's my hand,"* Ferdinand says. Miranda answers: *"And mine, with my heart in it."*

Ms Redman, flicking back her luscious hair, suggested the following moves. Jamie holds out his hand on, *"Here is my hand."* I take his hand on, *". . . and mine, with my heart in it."* On the word *heart* I press his hand to my chest. (Dodgy!) He takes a step towards me and we kiss. (Oh no!) Then I push him away with the words: *"And now farewell till half an hour hence,"* and we exit in different directions.

"Do you think they *would* kiss at this stage?" I said. I was hoping to avoid any stage snogging. Couldn't we just hold hands like it said in the script?

"I'm sure they would," Doe said, laughing. "They're young. They're in love. No one is watching. Why? Are you feeling shy?"

"No," I said, feeling myself blush. If only she *knew*.

We ran the move. His hand . . . my hand . . . his hand on my chest (I steered it to the bony bit around my collar bone rather than my actual boobs) . . . step forward . . . and the kiss. It was the first time I'd kissed him in three months. I went all stiff and tense and my heart was pounding. As his lips came towards mine, I willed myself not to enjoy it. But I failed. The kiss felt warm and familiar. I felt myself soften, like ice melting.

After the rehearsal Jamie wanted to walk me home.

Take off the cloak, I told myself. You're Isabel now.

"I'm fine," I said. "I was going to catch the bus."

"I'll walk you to the bus stop, then," he said. He was oozing charm. He touched my elbow as we went through the door.

"Won't Kirsty mind?" I said.

"We're only walking," he said, with a sexy grin. "Anyway, no one said we couldn't be friends." Friends? Was that what we were? I hadn't noticed. I said nothing.

There was a chilly breeze outside. I buttoned my jacket.

"What do you think of the play?" he asked, as we passed through the school gates.

"I think Miranda's a bit wet," I said.

"You're very good," he said. "Perfect and peerless in fact." Was he taking the piss? I couldn't tell. We were passing the window of the eight-till-late shop. Jamie glanced at his reflection and instinctively touched his hair. No change there then. Still looking in mirrors.

"How's your mum?" Jamie said. I was caught off guard. Mum always really liked him – when we were going out together. He was quite flirty with her – which she found flattering – and always *so* polite. She was sad, when we split up.

"She's fine," I said. "Same as ever." We'd reached the bus stop. I put my bag down on the seat in the shelter.

"Shall we give it another go, Isabel?" Jamie said. Was he asking me out? I had my back to him when he said it. I was tempted to turn round and knee him in the nuts. The cheek of it!

"I don't think so," I said with more than a hint of sarcasm.

"We were good together," he said. What a cliché! Was he always that unoriginal?

"That's not what you said when you dumped me,"

I said. My bus was coming round the corner. Thank God! I picked up my bag.

"Think about it," he said, as I put out my hand to stop the bus.

"No Jamie," I said. I didn't look at him as I stepped onboard. I didn't dare.

Act II Scene ii

Lights up on a room in Isabel's house. Isabel, dressed in Winnie-the-Pooh pyjamas, is lying on the sofa watching TV.

ISABEL:

Macy phoned me while I was watching *Friends*.

"He said *what*?" she shrieked.

I told her again. "He said, 'Shall we give it another go, Isabel?' I kid you not!"

"And you told him where to get off, I hope," Macy said.

"Absolutely," I said. "Tosser!" I added, for effect. Even as I said it I remembered him kissing me. But that wasn't Jamie, it was Ferdinand. And I wasn't Isabel, was I? I was Miranda. Same lips though. Same warm sweet lips.

"I wish I had hair like Jennifer Aniston," I said, changing the subject.

"Stuff Jennifer Aniston! Mrs Brad Pitt! Your hair's great," Macy said.

"Perfect and peerless," I said.

"Sorry?" said Macy.

"It's a line that Ferdinand says," I said. "To

Miranda. And Jamie said it on the way to the bus stop."

"Ex-*cuse* me?" said Macy in her now-hang-on-a-minute-let's-get-this-straight voice. "He said *what*?"

"He said I was perfect and peerless," I said, "as Miranda."

"Oh p-*lease*!" said Macy, disgusted.

"Have you done your French homework?" I said. I was trying to steer the conversation away from my love life. Lately that seems to be all Macy wants to talk about. It didn't work.

"Any more news from Dunkin Donuts?" she said.

"No," I said. "Anyway, I only posted *my* letter to him on Wednesday."

"Wednesday, Thursday, Friday..." Macy was counting up the days. "He should have gotten it today, then," she said.

"I only put a second class stamp on it," I said.

"You stingy mare!" Macy said.

"Look," I said. "If you're so interested in Duncan Muck-Cloud why don't *you* write to him?"

"Maybe I will," she said. "See you, babe."

She'd talked through so much of the *Friends* episode that I'd lost the plot, so I flossed my teeth and went to bed.

Act II Scene iii

Monday, early morning. Enter Isabel in purple fluffy dressing gown and Scooby Doo slippers. She looks at the post on the doormat and picks up a small hand-written envelope. It is addressed to her. Tearing it open, Isabel reads:

Dear Isabel (or shall I call you Izzy?)

It was great to get your letter. I'm glad to hear your message-in-a-bottle wasn't a serious plea for help. So you're not a damsel in distress after all. What a relief.

Sorry if – by finding your message – I have prevented you from starting a beautiful relationship with a fish! Fish are overrated in my opinion. My dad spends half his life pursuing them, but frankly they're not great company. They're no fun at parties. No conversation.

So . . . you're in *The Tempest*! That's another bizarre coincidence. *The Tempest* is one of my A-Level texts and I love it. It's my favourite play. All that stuff about wild islands and stormy seas . . . I don't think Miranda's a drip, she's just innocent –

kind of otherworldly. I picture her as a bit of a hippy chick – all seaweed and shells and a bit spaced out. Like a mermaid on Prozac!

As for Macy, she sounds seriously scary! Which character is she playing? Not Caliban, I hope. Write and tell me all about it.

Do you have e-mail? Here's my e-mail address in case you do: Poshporpoise@hotmail.com See you in cyberspace, maybe?

Yours, Duncan

PS I can't compete in the Pets-Win-Prizes department. Cleopatra sounds wicked! We have a dog called Boris who stinks of seaweed and barks at his own shadow and a mad goat (nameless) that eats our rubbish!

Act II Scene iv

Curtain rises. Isabel sits at a study booth in the school library. She is writing in an A4 notebook with a silver hologramic pen.

ISABEL:

Miranda only has four scenes which – considering she's the female lead – is a bit on the skimpy side. Ms Redman says *The Tempest* was Shakespeare's last play, so maybe he'd just run out of lines.

We have to keep a rehearsal diary as part of our Performing Arts coursework. I'm trying to write in it after each rehearsal while it's still fresh in my mind. Tonight we did the blocking for this weird scene in Act IV. Prospero tells Ferdinand and Miranda that they have his blessing as a couple but that they mustn't sleep together before they get married. (How nosy is that?) Then he magics up some spirits – Kirsty Baker among them – who act out a pageant about love and fertility. Everyone is happy until Prospero remembers that Caliban, with two shipwrecked men – Trinculo, a jester, and Stephano, a drunken butler – are on their way to murder Prospero and take over the island. Everyone apart from Prospero leaves the stage in a hurry.

Ferdinand and Miranda don't really do anything in the scene apart from sit there and watch the pageant and I only have one line to say – about how furious Prospero looks: *"Never till this day, saw I him touched with anger so distempered."*

Ms Redman wants to get a contrast between the summer feel of the pageant – lots of flowers and ribbons and Maypole dancing – and the dark tone of the rest of the scene. Prospero has a speech at the end: *"Our revels now are ended"*, that Ms Redman says is about the magic of a play dissolving away to leave the grim reality that: *"We are such stuff as dreams are made on and our little lives are rounded with a sleep."* In other words, life doesn't add up to much and anyway, we're all going to die. Cheery stuff! Maybe Shakespeare was feeling especially old and weary when he wrote that bit!

Kirsty Baker wasn't very good. She was wooden and her lines sounded like she was reading them – which she was, despite having had two weeks to learn them and only one scene to learn. Do I sound bitter? Do you blame me? Kirsty looked a mess too, which is unusual for her. Normally, she looks like she's spent three hours in the mirror doing her make-up. She's got immaculately plucked eyebrows and perfectly manicured nail extensions.

Jamie was pretty offhand with Kirsty at the

rehearsal. He hardly spoke to her in the breaks. I wondered if she knew he'd asked me out on Friday night. While we were running the scene Jamie kept offering me swigs from his can of Dr Pepper. I hate Dr Pepper but I drank it just to wind up Kirsty. One of Iris (Kirsty Baker)'s lines is about the true love of *"the blest lovers"*. She's talking about Ferdinand and Miranda. *"Blest lovers"*. That must have really stuck in her throat.

I had loads of homework to do after the rehearsal. I had a whole French essay – "Examine the theme of religious hypocrisy in Moliere's *Tartuffe*" – and notes to make for English on Tennyson's view of love – " *'Tis better to have loved and lost than never to have loved at all . . .*" Is that a fact?

It was gone eleven when I'd finished it all. Nevertheless I e-mailed Duncan. Just a quickie. Why not? The guy is lonely.

  To: <u>Poshporpoise@hotmail.com</u>
    Subject: Address
    Dear Duncan
    Thanx for your letter. What's with the porpoises? Yes, I've got e-mail. As you'll see from this message my address is <u>madizzy@fish.co.uk</u> Can't get away from those fish! I'm relieved that you're an expert on *The*

Tempest. I'm floundering (more fish) a bit.
What's it *about*?
Tell all.
Cheers, Isabel

Act II Scene v

Isabel's bedroom, Friday evening. Isabel sits on the bed in her underwear, her hair in a towel turban, a pale green face mask on her face. She is writing in a notebook.

ISABEL:

We blocked the last scene (V:i) in drama lesson today. Everything gets sorted out in a grand tidy-up. Having brought his enemies to the island and scared the life out of them, Prospero tells them he forgives them for all the wicked things they've done. The king (Rosie Mason with a stick-on beard) thinks that Ferdinand (his son) has drowned but then Prospero pulls back a curtain and there – as if by magic – are Ferdinand and Miranda. And guess what they're doing? Playing chess! Can you believe that? Newly in love and they're playing chess! It will be cocoa and Scrabble in front of the telly next! Get a life, Miranda!

Miranda looks up from the chessboard and sees all these people – more humans than she's ever seen: Prospero, and King Alonso, and the king's brother Sebastian, and nasty Uncle Antonio, and Gonzalo the good guy, and two people called Adrian and Francisco that don't say very much – and she says her best line in the whole play: *"How beauteous mankind is! O brave new world that has such people in't!"* Brave New World. There's book called that. I think Pete's got a copy of it, on the bookshelf halfway up the stairs.

Finally Gonzalo makes a speech about finding lost things – lost sons, lost kingdoms and lost selves – and everyone makes plans to leave the island and go home. By amazing coincidence, the ship which Miranda watched being wrecked at the beginning of the play appears, good as new. Prospero gives Ariel his freedom. And that's the end. Final curtain. Lots of clapping. So it *is* a happy ending. Must remember to tell Pete.

So now we've blocked the whole play – and it's starting to make sense. I've managed to learn most of my lines too. On Saturday we've got a special all-day workshop, so I'll have to miss dancing and my singing lesson – and next week we start polishing the scenes. I can't believe we're halfway through the rehearsal period already!

Isabel washes the green face mask off her face and blow-dries her hair.

I was getting ready for a night out. It was Chloe Stretton's seventeenth birthday party. Macy arrived about eight. She had glitter on her cheekbones and black leather jeans on.

"Disco diva!" I said, giving her a kiss. "Which top?" I held up two tops on hangers, one in each hand.

"Just go in your bra," said Macy. "You'll look like Geri Halliwell."

"Oh cheers," I said. I was waiting for a proper answer. Macy looked at me and narrowed her eyes.

"The white one," she said.

Pete gave us a lift. Chloe's house was a couple of kilometres away. I hadn't been there before. The house was right next to a big dark church and it was huge.

"The Old Vicarage," said Pete, reading the sign on the gatepost.

"It looks like something out of the Addams' Family," Macy said.

There was a graveyard just over the garden wall.

"Spooky," I said, ringing the bell.

Chloe answered the door.

"Hope we're not too early," I said.

"No, there's loads of people here," she said.

"Happy birthday," said Macy, and she gave Chloe a CD wrapped in silver paper.

"It's from both of us," I said. "Happy birthday!"

Most of the drama group was there and a load of Chloe's friends from the design and tech crowd. Chloe's in the play. She's my nasty Uncle Antonio – not that she looks much like my uncle. Her hair is dyed a bright plum colour and she wears lots of leather and fake fur, but she is tall – and what my mum would call "statuesque". Put her in a big coat and a wig and she could just about pass for a bloke!

"Do you want a drink?" Chloe said. We followed her into the kitchen. It was vast and painted bright yellow. All around the walls were shelves full of pots and jars and big Mexican plates.

"Great room," I said.

"Great smell," said Macy.

"Mum made a chilli," Chloe said.

Oh no, not more chilli! There was a huge pan on the cooker and bowls of bread and salad on the table.

"They've left a piddly amount of beer," Chloe said, pointing to about a dozen cans on the table, "because Mum said she didn't want to come back to pools of vomit. But there's loads of Coke and Seven Up and –" she lifted an almost empty bottle and shook it "– a teeny drop of Irn Bru. There *was* some cider, but it seems to have disappeared."

"Coke's fine," I said. The workshop started at ten the next morning. I didn't want a hangover.

We walked along the hall to the sitting-room. It was painted blood red. Chloe had turned the lights down low and people were dancing to some hip-hop. I put my drink down on the mantelpiece and joined in. Macy danced with me. She's a great dancer. Lots of Latin American bum wiggle.

It must have been about ten when Jamie and Kirsty arrived. They didn't look too happy. He was all denim and hair gel but no cheesy smile. She had smudged lipstick and she looked like she'd been crying. They sat down on a sofa in the corner. She was holding on to his arm and scowling, pressing her face against his shoulder.

I was dancing to Jamiroquai. The room was red-hot and I was getting seriously sweaty. I could feel Jamie's eyes on me. I went in search of water.

Someone had opened the back door and a delicious breeze was wafting into the kitchen. I filled a glass from the tap and went outside. The garden was dark and creepy. As my eyes adjusted to the darkness I could see a stone path leading away from the house, between some tall bushes. I walked along it through an archway where trailing leaves brushed against my scalp. The cool air felt lovely on my damp skin. A cat jumped across the path, making me start. I could feel the hair standing up on the back of my neck. Beyond the arch there was a pond. Suddenly a big moon came out from behind the clouds and caught the surface of the pond in a flash of silver. Beside the pond was a bench – and there was someone sitting on it. I could just make out a bulky shape silhouetted against the navy sky. I stopped and stood still, my heart pounding. The shape turned to face me.

"Who's that?" it said. I recognized the voice.

"Isabel," I said.

"Izzy," it said. "Come and join me." It was Andy Shaw – Caliban, the man monster.

I sat down on the bench beside him. He looked rough – even in the dark. He was swigging beer from a can.

"Do you want a drink?" he said, holding it out to me.

"No thanks," I said. "I'm on water." I raised my glass. "Cheers," I said.

"Sensible Izzy," said Andy. "I've had too much to drink." He reached down to his feet. On the path beside them was a plastic cider bottle. He picked it up and waved it in my face. It was empty. So *that* was where it went!

"Are you enjoying the party, Izzy?" said Andy.

"Yeah," I said. I was, up until that point – in a limited sort of way.

"Are you happy Izzy?" he said. "I mean, *really* happy?" He let out a huge belch. "Excuse me," he said, patting my leg. I slid – discreetly, so as not to hurt his feelings – away from him along the bench so that my leg was out of reach.

"How do you mean?" I said. *Was* I happy? That was a bit of a big question. Andy's really into life's big questions. Especially when he's drunk. "I think so," I said.

"Is there a god?" he said. Like I said, the bigger the question, the better. That's philosophy students for you.

"I don't know," I said again, a bit non-committally. I looked at the house. The lights were shining out brightly and I could hear music and voices. What was Jamie doing, I wondered? As if I was bothered.

"Nietzsche says God is dead," Andy said, swaying on the bench. *Who the hell was Nietzche anyway?*

"He was bluffing," I said. "I think I'd better make you a coffee." I took hold of Andy's arm. Andy stood up and then, with one lurching step forward, he was sick into the pond. I covered my nose and waited till he'd finished wretching, then I said, "Nice treat for the fish."

"I'll be wise hereafter," Andy said as he staggered towards the house. *"And seek for grace."* Caliban says that after Prospero has punished him. *I'll be wise hereafter* . . . Fat chance.

I left Andy falling asleep on a couch in the dining-room and headed back to the dancing. Macy met me in the hall with a bowl of chilli in her hands.

"The chilli's great!" she said. "Shall I get you some?"

"No thanks," I said. "It looks too much like Andy's puke!"

"Gross!" Macy said.

* * *

In the blood-red room Phil Colvin was headbanging to *My Way* by Limp Biskit. The air seemed to be full of steam and there was a rank smell from too many bodies in too small a space. I didn't fancy it much, so I headed back to the kitchen. Sebastian Reeves handed me a bowl of Doritos. I took it and wandered into the dining-room, nibbling them. Andy Shaw was fast asleep with his mouth open. Jamie walked in, eating a bread stick. There was no sign of Kirsty.

"Hello Miranda," he said.

"It's Isabel actually," I said. He smiled.

"So, how's life?" he said, biting his bread stick.

"Fantastic," I said, looking away. Was *he* going to ask me if I was happy too? "I'm just going to get some food," I said, stepping past him.

In the kitchen Chloe was wiping up a glass of Coke that someone had spilled near the cooker. The Doritos had made me thirsty. I filled a pint glass with water and drank it down in one.

"Damn!" said Chloe, suddenly. "We forgot the spuds!" She opened the oven door and there were about thirty baked potatoes all wizened and wrinkly.

"I'll have one," I said. She lifted one out.

"Ah shit! It's hot!" she said. What did she expect?

The potato was almost hollow inside. I heaped some salad on to it, picked up a fork and went back to the sitting-room. The music was Whitney Houston now. Chloe was certainly catering for all musical tastes! Macy was slow-dancing with Phil Colvin. Thick rivers of sweat were running down his T-shirt and his bleached hair was standing up in spikes. Macy's head was level with his stomach because she's so tiny. She was singing along to: "*And I . . . will always love you . . .*" She caught my eye and winked. Then Jamie appeared in the doorway.

"What's this?" he said. "The karaoke room?" Macy gave him a dirty look and went on singing. Jamie was walking towards me. Any minute now he was going to ask me to dance. I needed an excuse to leave.

"Where's the loo?" I said to Chloe. She was dancing with a guy in black nail varnish.

"Upstairs, second on the right," she shouted.

The bathroom door was locked. I knocked but no one answered so I sat down on the landing floor with my back to a radiator and waited. "*My father is hard at study. Pray now rest yourself . . .*" I said. One of the good things about learning lines is it gives you an excuse to talk to yourself. "*How beauteous mankind is. O brave new world that has such people in't.*" I noticed there was an orange splash mark on my top. I hoped it was chilli and not sick. The bathroom door was still shut. My glass of water had worked fast and I was getting desperate. After ten minutes I knocked again.

"Hello," I said. "Anyone there?" Someone turned on a tap and I heard splashing in the sink. I pressed my ear to the door. There was a faint sound of sobbing.

"Hello," I said, knocking louder. "Open the door! I need a pee!"

"Who's that?" a voice said.

"Isabel!" I said. "Do you think you could hurry up?"

I heard a bolt slide back and the door opened very slowly. There was Kirsty Baker, her face puffed up like a red balloon, her eye make-up run across her cheeks and a look of complete misery on her face. How could I not feel sorry for her?

"I hate him!" she blurted out. "I hate his guts."

No prizes for guessing who.

"Can I come in before I wet my pants?" I said. I stepped into the bathroom. Kirsty showed no sign of going so I locked the door again and sat down on the loo. Kirsty slumped on to the floor, her back against the side of the bath, her head in her hands.

"Has he dumped you?" I said. She nodded. So now she knew what it felt like. At least he'd done it to her face.

"I knew he would," she sobbed. "I could feel it coming."

More than I could, I thought.

"It's because of you," she said, looking at me with

wild eyes. "He's still in love with you." I thought of *Fatal Attraction*. Was she about to pull out a knife and stab me? We *were* in a bathroom, after all.

"He's not in love with me," I said, unrolling the toilet paper. "He's in love with himself."

She ignored me. "He talks about you all the time," she said. "How good you are in the play. How good you are at dancing. What good shape you're in. You've always been better than me – at everything!" She let out a howl of despair and buried her head in her hands.

Did she really hate me? Had she always been jealous of me? Ever since we were four? Since I was the Virgin Mary in the Christmas play and she was a camel? I was tempted to unlock the bathroom door and run but I couldn't. That would be too cruel. I tried to think of something comforting to say that didn't sound fake.

"You've got great hair," I said feebly. "Mine's like straw!" I looked in the mirror and pulled a face at myself. Was that the best I could do? I flushed the loo.

"Who gives a shit about hair?" Kirsty said with a monumental sniff.

"Here," I said. I handed her a wadge of toilet paper and she blew her nose. "He's not worth it," I said. "You're well shot of him." That was what everyone had said to me. Macy and Alice. Even Mum and Pete.

"Hmmph," Kirsty grunted.

"Look," I said, glancing at my watch. "It's half-eleven. We're getting a lift soon. Macy's dad's coming. I turn into a pumpkin if I stay out after midnight. Do you want us to give you a lift home?"

"Thanks," she said, sniffing again. She stood up and straightened her clothes. I licked my finger and wiped a smear of eye shadow off her cheek. She smiled at me. Maybe she didn't hate me so much. Then, all of a sudden, she gave me a hug. A hug! Kirsty Baker!

"Thanks, Isabel," she said, burying her face in my shoulder. Then, with another sob, she said, "I wish I was you!"

"Don't wish that," I said, gently unfastening her arms from my neck. "It's not that great."

When I got home I looked in my bedroom mirror. Not only did my white top still have a mysterious orange stain on the front, it now had Kirsty's lipstick and mascara daubed across the shoulder too. Cheers everyone! It was midnight but I didn't feel tired. I switched on the computer and started to take off my make-up while it booted up. I had mail. There was a little yellow envelope. One message unread: *Duncan: Porpoises!* I clicked to open it.

Dear Isabel

About porpoises – they're a bit like dolphins, only smaller and browner with sleek oily bodies. They hang about in big groups – twenty or thirty at a time. When I go out in my dad's boat, off the point, out west of the island, we sometimes see them. Just after the tide has turned is the best time. They move past the boat like a troupe of dancers – like acrobats – all going the same way, tumbling in great slow-motion cartwheels. They're *so* cool!

About *The Tempest* – it's about going mad on an island, and power, and freedom, and magic, and storms, and transformation, and forgiveness, and love at first sight.

Yours
Duncan

I smiled and clicked "reply".

Dear Duncan

Thanx for the info re *Tempest* and porpoises. I don't see many marine mammals in Greater Manchester. No fish either.

I've just been to a rank party. When I said I liked parties, I didn't mean the kind of party where you provide moral support while a drunk philosophy student throws up in a garden pond, or the sort where you end up with the latest victim of the git who is the former love of your life crying on your shoulder in the bathroom. Not my kind of fun!

Yours cheesed-off-edly

Isabel

Act II Scene vi

The drama studio. Saturday morning. Enter Isabel in a tie-dyed top and embroidered jeans. She is eating a banana.

ISABEL:

It was ten-thirty by the time most of the group arrived the next day. Andy Shaw wasn't there at all. Kirsty Baker looked like she wished she wasn't. Ms Redman was looking dynamic – crisp white cotton shirt, cargo pants, no shoes, bottle of water in hand.

"OK, let's start before we waste any more time," she said. "I'd like to introduce Cal . . ." She gestured to the man standing beside her. "Cal's a professional actor. He's worked in the theatre. He's done TV and film too. Some of you might have seen him in *A Midsummer Night's Dream* at the Royal Exchange last year." Macy nodded. "He's very kindly agreed to work with you all today. So, welcome Cal!"

Cal was about fifty – lean and wiry, bald head, tanned face, bursting with energy. He had bare feet too and a T-shirt with holes in it that said "Will

Power" with a faded picture of Shakespeare's face on the front.

"Welcome too, to Mr Kempe," said Doe with a swish of her hair, "who's very generously given up his Saturday to join us." Mr Kempe is an English teacher at our school. He looks like Sting only a bit younger. Macy had a big crush on him in Year Eleven.

"Sacrifices for art," said Mr Kempe with a smile. He winked at Ms Redman.

"What's *he* doing here?" Macy hissed.

"Giving up his Saturday," I whispered.

Macy was avoiding Phil Colvin, who kept smiling lecherously at her. After the slow-dancing things had got a bit heavy between them. I think, in the cold light of day, she'd thought better of it. Phil's not really her type. He's a Slipknot fan for starters.

"Cal's going to begin with a physical warm-up," Doe said.

"Hi!" said Cal, springing forward. "If you could all take your shoes off . . ."

"As if!" said Chloe Stretton. She's surgically attached to her purple Doc Marten boots. Reluctantly she sat on the floor and unlaced them.

The warm-up was pretty strenuous – jogging on the spot, bending, arm-circling, bouncing about like kangaroos. Cal even had us dragging ourselves across the floor like snakes. Some of the cast got the giggles. I was pretty warm after twenty minutes and

I'm used to two hours of dance on a Saturday morning. Sebastian Reeves was red in the face.

"OK, well done," said Cal, clapping his hands. "Take a break ... Why do we do warm-ups?" He glanced around the room with a wild birdlike stare.

"God knows!" said Chloe Stretton. Everyone laughed.

"To get fit," said Sebastian Reeves. Beads of sweat studded his forehead.

"Yeah," said Cal, putting his hands on his hips. "Actors need to be fit to move well – to push their bodies to the limits."

"I wish!" said Macy under her breath.

"To be supple," I said. Siobhan's always talking about suppleness.

"Yep," Cal said. "We also need to be supple and flexible. We're acting with our whole bodies. Not just from the neck up."

"To make fools of ourselves?" said Natalie Roberts. Everyone laughed again.

"That's not as daft as it seems," said Cal. "Theatre's all about trust. We need to lose our inhibitions and trust each other if we're going to perform well as a team."

I looked at Mr Kempe. He was looking at Doe. She'd done the warm-up too and she had damp wisps of hair around her face.

"We're going to warm up our voices now," Cal

declared. "So find a space and lie on your backs!" We did lots of deep breathing and humming and letting our breath out to an "ooh" sound or an "ay" sound.

"Put your hands on your rib cage," said Cal, "and feel your lungs emptying and filling. Deep breaths, right down to your diaphragm."

I thought about what Mr O'Leary says about singing from the pit of your stomach.

"Now come and sit in a circle," Cal said. He gave us all a strip of paper with a number and some words on it. Mine said: "*8 All the mice go Clang.*" Macy's said: "*5 Where the trees go Ping.*"

"What the heck?" said Natalie Roberts.

"This is a nonsense rhyme by Spike Milligan called *On the Ning Nang Nong*," said Cal.

"That's *my* line," said Chloe Stretton. "*On the Ning Nang Nong* . . . Look!" She pointed proudly to her strip of paper. Doe smiled.

"We're going to use the words of the poem for a number of things," Cal said. "To warm up our voices – which is essential for any perfoming. To develop rhythm skills, and to work on timing and listening. We're also going to have a bit of fun!" Across the circle Natalie pulled a face at me. "I've given you the lines in a random order," Cal said, "so the first thing we're going to do is run it line by line. So, if you have number one, you start. Number two follows on, and so on. Do you get the idea?"

"Kind of," said Phil Colvin. He was grining at Macy. She gave me an "Oh-my-God!" look.

We staggered through the poem, line by line . . .

"It's you," Sebastian Reeves said pompously to Sara Bottomley, nudging her in the ribs.

"How d'you know?" she said.

"Because you're line six and that was line five. You have to count."

"Oops, soz," said Sara. "*And the teapots Jibber Jabber Joo*," she said. "What's *that* supposed to mean?"

"It's nonsense," said Doe.

"It's worse than Shakespeare," said Natalie.

"Can I do my line please?" said Sebastian. "*On the Nong Ning Nang . . .*" he said, pronouncing each word very precisely.

"*All the mice go Clang*," I answered.

"*And you just can't catch them when they do*," said Kirsty Baker with a very unamused face.

When we finally reached the end of the rhyme Cal said, "That was *abysmal*! I thought you were supposed to be drama students!"

He looked at Doe, who said, "Don't blame me! I've only been teaching them for three weeks!" She was sitting on the rostra with Mr Kempe.

"Again then," said Cal. "And let's try to get a bit of a beat going." He snapped his fingers energetically. We did it three more times, getting faster and faster. By the third attempt it was *almost* rhythmical.

"OK," said Cal, clapping. "Let's add some movement. When you speak, you stand up tall like toy soldiers. When you've finished, you flop to the floor like a rag doll. Everyone in a crouching position please . . ."

We made it to line seven, then Natalie Roberts got the giggles and fell over, and the whole thing collapsed. We tried again and got to line twelve. On the third attempt we got it right, all the way to the last line, which was Jamie Burrows.

"Is the Ning Nang Ning Nang Nong!" Jamie said, and he punched the air in triumph.

"Thank God!" said Cal.

After that it got *really* silly. We had to memorize our line, crawl around the floor whispering it, roll about the floor singing it, run from one end of the studio to the other and then shout it – and I thought the things Mr O'Leary made me do were daft! When Cal shouted "Scatter!" we had to dash to somewhere in the studio and pretend to hide – pressed against the wall, or up on the rostra, or under a chair. From there we had to say the whole poem, line by line, listening out for our cue line and shouting at the tops of our voices as if it was an emergency. Imagine yelling *All the mice go Clang!* as if it was an urgent announcement!

Finally we had to arrange ourselves in a "body sculpture" on the rostra blocks and perform the poem to Doe and Mr Kempe. I was kneeling on the ground and Macy was resting her elbows on my shoulders. Phil Colvin was lying on the ground in front of me, with his feet on the back of Natalie Roberts who was curled in a ball like a mushroom float. "That's wonderful!" Cal shouted. "Freeze it! And . . . from the top!"

We ran the whole poem without a hitch:

"On the Ning Nang Nong"
"Where the cows go Bong!"
"And the monkeys all say Boo!"
"There's a Nong Nang Ning"
"Where the trees go Ping!"
"And the teapots Jibber Jabber Joo."
"On the Nong Ning Nang"
"All the mice go Clang!"
"And you just can't catch 'em if they do!"
"So it's Ning Nang Nong!"
"Cows go Bong!"
"Nong Ning Nang!"
"The mice go Clang!"
"What a noisy place to belong,"
"Is the Ning Nang Ning Nang Nong!"

"Bravo!" Doe shouted. She clapped enthusiastically and Mr Kempe wolf-whistled and stamped his feet. "OK, take a break!" Doe shouted. "Back in ten minutes. I want to talk to you about costumes."

I went with Macy out into the corridor to get a drink from the vending machine. Phil and Jamie were there.

"What a complete nutter!" said Phil, edging up close to Macy.

"He's cool," Macy said. "I love his voice. It's *so* sexy!" Phil looked disappointed.

Jamie bought a Mars Bar from the machine. "Do you think she'll make us wear tights?" he said to Phil.

"I wouldn't put it past her. The woman's a closet sadist, bringing that mad bugger in!" Phil nodded towards the studio door. "Nong Nang Ning!" he said with disgust. "How old does he think we are?"

"I think he's fantastic," I said. Jamie glanced at me.

"I saw him in *A Midsummer Night's Dream*," Macy said. "He played Bottom."

"Arse, more like!" said Phil, and they both burst out laughing.

"Well he's not playing *my* bottom," said Jamie. Phil gave a snort of laughter and they went off down the corridor laughing about bottoms and arses and all those things boys find so amusing.

"I can never understand why British people find bottoms *so* funny!" said Macy, snapping the ring-pull on a Diet Coke.

"British *men*!" I said. "Don't include *me*!"

"I wonder if Dunkin Donuts is into toilet humour?" Macy said.

"Write and ask him," I said.

I hadn't told Macy about the e-mails. It wasn't that I didn't trust her. I just didn't want her to get the wrong end of the stick and go on about him all the time.

We were just starting to talk about costumes when Andy Shaw finally arrived. Everyone cheered. Andy put his hands over his ears and winced. "Not so loud," he said.

"Afternoon, Andy," said Doe. "I hear you had a good night last night."

"Did I?" groaned Andy. He pulled up a chair.

"We were just talking about costumes," she said. "But don't worry, you don't get one. You'll be stark naked and covered in mud!" She turned to Cal. "He's Caliban," she explained. Cal nodded knowingly.

"Naked?" said Andy disbelievingly. "Isn't that illegal?"

"Well perhaps not totally naked," Doe said with a grin. "We might give you a pair of Y-fronts."

"Not Y-fronts!" Andy said. "Spare me the shame of that! Boxers or nothing!"

Doe told us what she was thinking of, costume-wise. "Timeless modern," she said. Definitely not period dress, so no doublet and hose or long frocks with hooped petticoats. "Everything in shades of blue and grey," she said, "to suggest the sea. And I want the fabric to look washed and weathered – as if it's been in the sea and then dried in the sun. So we can have some fun with dye and bleach."

"Can I have shells in my hair?" I said. "You know, sort of island hippy chick? Glastonbury by the sea?"

"That's a nice idea," Doe said.

"How about we wrap you in seaweed and give you a mermaid's tail too," said Macy sarcastically.

"OK," I said. "As long as Macy can wear silver Lycra!"

"And swing in on a wire!" Macy laughed.

"What about my magic cloak?" Sebastian said. "Prospero's got to have a cloak."

"Isabel, I wondered if that was a project for you – in textiles?" Doe said.

"Yeah, great," I said. Now she tells me! When the opening night is less than a month away!

"Shame Jamie doesn't get to wear tights," said Macy, later. "He'd have looked a right jerk!"

Jamie was being very cool towards me. I wondered if he'd finally got the message I wasn't interested in re-opening old wounds. Kirsty Baker was giving him a wide berth. She stuck like a limpet to Sara Bottomley for the whole day and looked whey-faced and pale. I bet *Ning Nang Nong* was just what she needed, poor girl!

We spent the afternoon working in two groups – principal characters with Cal in the studio, everyone else in the hall with Doe to work on the maypole dance. We were working on what Cal called "pair bonding".

"Sounds dodgy," said Macy, raising her eyebrows.

Cal put us in pairs, depending on who our character spends most time with on stage. So yes, I was with Jamie – Miranda and Ferdinand. Prospero was with Ariel, Stephano with Trinculo and so on. Only Andy Shaw (Caliban) was left without a partner.

"Story of my life," he said. "Don't worry. I'll just sit in a corner and snooze."

But then Mr Kempe – or Rich as he told us to call him, seeing as though it was out of hours – volunteered to be his partner.

"I didn't know you cared, sir," Andy said in a camp voice.

With our partner we had to "build trust". *That's a tall order, Cal*, I wanted to say. *This guy broke my heart!* Most of Cal's trust-building was very touchy feely. I had to shut my eyes and fall backwards into Jamie's arms. He had to lead me blindfolded round an obstacle course. We both had to join hands, lean back and balance like a see-saw. Then we had to choose a line from the play and whisper it to each other as one person rubbed the other's shoulders. How intimate did he want us to *get*? More intimate than that, obviously! The next thing we had to do was sit cross-legged on the floor, facing each other, touch noses and then say the line to each other. Jamie and I used to do this Eskimo kissing thing that was alarmingly similar. I couldn't help thinking about it. Too close for comfort or what? I wondered how Macy was getting on rubbing noses with Sebastian Reeves! Which was worse? Getting cosy with someone you definitely didn't fancy, or getting cosy with someone you did fancy? *Did* fancy – that's *did* in the past tense.

However, if I said I didn't enjoy all this up-close-and-personal stuff with Jamie Burrows at all, I would be lying. I also couldn't help noticing that now that he wasn't coming on to me any more, I felt more interested in him. Why had he stopped flirting with me? It wasn't because of Kirsty. She was yesterday's girl now, and anyway, she was out in the hall dancing about with a length of ribbon. Perhaps he'd only been showing interest in me to make her jealous? Did he *really* talk about me all the time, like Kirsty said? Was he *really* still in love with me?

"*I beyond all limit of what else i'th'world, do love, prize, honour you,*" said Ferdinand, his nose brushing against mine.

"*I'll be your servant whether you will or no,*" Miranda said back to him.

"Well done, you two," said Cal, patting my shoulder. "That was very convincing. I could almost believe you were in love for real!"

"Oh, give me a break!" said Macy behind me.

Act II Scene vii

Isabel's house. Saturday night. Enter Macy from stage right, clutching a Blockbuster Video box and a family-size bag of toffee popcorn.

ISABEL:

"Look what I got!" Macy said. "A movie called *Message in a Bottle*! What d'ya know?" She waved the video box in my face.

We went into the sitting room. I'd made us tall glasses of orange and carrot juice with Mum's new juicer.

"The box described it as a touching romantic comedy," Macy said. "The guy in the store said it was a weepy chick-flick!" She sucked the juice through a straw. "Yum! That tastes healthy! Here's some popcorn to spoil the effect!"

The guy in the shop was right. Kevin Costner – looking like Tony Blair – sends love letters (in bottles, thrown into the sea) to his dead wife Catherine. Sad, divorced, single-parent journalist Theresa (Robin Penn something or other) finds one washed up on the shore. Theresa manages to trace where it's come from with the help of her newspaper (who go and

publish the letter), and she goes in search of Kevin C
– who, it turns out, is a lonely boat builder who lives
by a gorgeous beach. They fall in love (of course!).
She goes home to Chicago (and her son). Kevin C
visits her. They fall out. He goes home to his beach.
She follows him but concludes that he's still in love
with his dead wife, so she leaves again. He realizes
he's in love with her after all and writes one last letter
to his wife to explain that he's found someone new
to love. He then goes out in his new boat but a storm
comes. In the storm he goes to the rescue of a family
in a capsized boat and drowns saving them.

"I can't believe he *drowned*!" Macy said, blowing
her nose. "Life is *so* unfair! God!" There was a mound
of soggy tissues on the sofa between us. "So the moral
of the story, Isabel," she said, slurping the last drops
of her juice noisily through the straw, "is don't take
too long falling in love or Dunkin Donuts might
drown in a storm!"

What *is* she like?

After she'd gone, I checked my e-mail. There was a
message from Duncan:

Dear Isabel
  **Sorry about the lousy party. My brother
Neil once got *so* drunk on Dad's whisky. He
was sick all over the dog, which made him**

smell worse than usual. (The dog that is, not Neil!) Personally I don't touch the stuff – whisky or vomit!

So how are rehearsals going? Have you learnt all your lines? Life is pretty much as usual here. I came second in a table-tennis tournament and won a tenner. Wow! The Posh Porpoises are deep into practising for a gig we're doing at the Island Centre (sort of a community hall) in November. Ned – my best mate – is our drummer. He's truly awful and never manages to stay in time. If he wasn't my mate I'd be tempted to sack him! Not that we'd find anyone better – there are only 58 people in our whole school!

A dead minke whale washed up on our beach last week. It's bigger than Dad's boat. It's starting to pong a bit. Bet you don't get many beached whales in the middle of Manchester.

Cheers!

Duncan

PS Was the-git-who-was-the-former-love-of-your-life anything to do with your message to the fish?

I replied straight away.

Dear Duncan,

Thanks for your news of smelly dogs, smelly puke and smelly rotting whales! They were just what I needed after a night pigging out on toffee popcorn! (Macy and I watched a video.)

I decided not to mention the name of the video. He might read too much into it.

Rehearsals are OK and yes, I now know all of Miranda's lines – not that she has many! We had this workshop thingy today (all day!) with this mad actor who looked a bit like Billy Whizz. (Do you have the *Beano* on your island?) He made us do all this embarrassing stuff – but that's drama for you. And I love it!

Doe – our drama teacher (don't ask me what Doe stands for!) – has asked me to make Prospero's cloak. As if I didn't have enough to do!

In answer to your question . . . yes, when we went to Ardnamurchan (and my sister Alice wrote the message) I'd been freshly dumped by Jamie Burrows – git extraordinaire. Sadly, he's playing Ferdinand, so there's no escaping him. *C'est la vie!*

Well, time for bed. Give my love to the porpoises – posh and not so posh. Yours, Izzy

PS Is there any chance you could send me some shells? Miranda fancies wearing them in her hair!

Act II Scene viii

Isabel sits on her bed writing her rehearsal diary.

ISABEL:

Today we rehearsed the long scene in Act I again. It was so much better than last time. I don't know how Sebastian remembers all those lines – he's got pages and pages of them.

Ms Redman had this ace idea for when Prospero's telling me how we came to be on the island. He's going to have a big photo album and as he tells me about each person – Antonio, and Alonso the king, and Gonzalo the kind old man – he's going to show me photos of them. As he points to each person, big slides will appear on the back wall so that the audience can see them too. Cool! Ms Redman's arranged a photo shoot for Friday lunchtime. She's asked Mr Kempe to take the photos. I think there's something going on between those two!

Macy sang her song, *"Full fathom five thy father lies . . ."* at the rehearsal. It was beautiful. She'd added a xylophone accompaniment that she worked out with Mrs Bateman, the head of Music. It sounded silvery and magical. Jamie did the bit where he follows the music and meets Miranda, as if he was bewitched – which really worked. If they're under Prospero's spell, and the whole thing is enchanted, they can't help themselves can they? Prospero says, *"They are both in either's powers."* But actually, they're both in *his* power – his and Ariel's.

Isabel closes her notebook and stretches her arms above her head.

Macy had to dash off after the rehearsal to a dentist's appointment.

"Do you want to go for a coffee?" Jamie asked me.

I couldn't think of a reason why not. "Sure," I said.

We went to Starbucks on St Ann's Square which used to be a favourite place of ours.

"Is it still mocha with extra whipped cream?" he said, getting his wallet out.

"Just the regular cappuccino," I said.

We went downstairs to the squashy sofas.

"It's going to be good," he said, putting two cups down on a low table. "The play, I mean."

"Yeah," I said. "Sebastian's brilliant."

"You're pretty good too," he said. I remembered what Kirsty had said: *"He talks about you all the time. How good you are in the play . . ."* I dipped my spoon in the cappuccino froth.

"I enjoyed Saturday," he said. "I thought it was going to be awful." Jamie likes acting but he's not as into it as I am. It's not an all-consuming passion for him.

"It was great," I said. Ms Redman had said the point of the workshop was to help us gel as a cast and it had worked. Things had felt different at today's rehearsal – like we'd all gone up a gear.

"*Ning Nang Nong* was a bit goofy," said Jamie with a smile. "I preferred the pair bonding, personally." He sipped his coffee. It left a foamy line across his top lip. I laughed.

"You've got a 'tache," I said. I reached across and wiped it with my napkin. I'm not sure why. It was a bit of a familiar thing to do. But then he *was* familiar. Scarily familiar.

Jamie touched his lip with his finger. He was looking at me. It was *that* look – the drowning one. I looked down at the marble table top.

"I'm sorry I ended it," he said. I stared at my cup. "Us, I mean," he said softly. "It was the worst mistake I ever made."

Was he *really* saying this? *Was* he still in love with me?

"It's in the past," I said with a shrug. Why did I say *that*? As though it was no big deal. As if I wasn't bothered.

"I miss you, Iz," he said.

I pictured Macy with arched are-you-kidding? eyebrows. Heard her saying, "Ex-*cuse* me?" Did he *really* miss me? Did I miss Jamie? I had done. At the start. Three months ago.

Macy had suggested we go for a sauna – all part of our get-in-tip-top-shape-for-the-show programme. Like the popcorn!

We had the sauna cabin to ourselves. Macy was lying flat on her back on the baking wooden boards. She was wearing a black bikini with a towel wrapped around her hair, turban-style. I sloshed a ladle of water on to the hot coals and they spat and hissed. There was a smell of pine and eucalyptus.

"Full fathom five thy father lies . . . those are pearls that were his eyes," Macy was singing. When I told her I'd seen Jamie she stopped singing and sat up.

"You're going to the *movies* with him?" she said incredulously.

"Not *just* him," I said. "There's a whole crowd going. It's very low key. Just friends. It's that new Tom Cruise film."

"I don't have a problem with the *film* Isabel, just with the company you're keeping! Izzy, you're playing with *fire!*"

She's *so* over the top. "It's not a big deal," I said. I pulled my knees up to my chest and rested my back against the wall. The wood was burning – almost too hot to touch. My arms were filmed with sweat. Yes, Jamie had invited me to the pictures. And yes, I'd agreed to go. So what? I *felt* like going.

"He's different," I said. "Nicer. More mature." Macy snorted with disgust. "You've never liked him, have you?" I said. Jamie and I were already an item when Macy came on the scene, when she came from the States halfway through Year Eleven. She was always sarcastic about him, always making wisecracks, always dissing him.

"He's shallow," she said, sitting up and crossing her legs as if she was doing yoga. "He's like . . . a shell. No, he's like . . . an Easter egg! All sparkly and nice on the outside and nothing inside. Hollow. Nothing there." She tossed her head and the towel slipped off. Damp black curls tumbled across her shoulders.

I shifted position – further away from the blazing coals.

"You don't know him like I do," I said.

"No, thank God!" said Macy.

My head was thumping from the heat.

"I'm going in the shower," I said, standing up. Then I said, "He reckons splitting up was a mistake."

"Mistake for him, maybe," Macy said, lying back and closing her eyes.

"Look, Macy, he said he was *sorry*!" I said, picking up my towel.

"That doesn't mean you have to *forgive* him, Isabel," Macy said.

I slammed the sauna door behind me.

Act II Scene ix

Macy's house. Tuesday night. Macy is plucking her
eyebrows in the bathroom mirror.

MACY:

Some people just never learn. I mean, why would
Isabel want to be in the same *room* with Jamie
Burrows, let alone snuggled up in some movie
theatre with him? The guy's poisonous. What is it
with her? A death wish or something?

Turns out she's been e-mailing Dunkin Donuts in
secret too. This girl should work out what she wants.
Seriously! I called in on my way back from singing.
Isabel had been kind of cool with me since she
flounced out of the sauna. She had all these shells in
her room. Like, where does she find shells in the
middle of Manchester?

"I got them on holiday," she says. "When I went to
Scotland."

"How come I've never seen them before?" I
say. There were loads of them – pointy ones like
sandcastles, and long flat blue ones, and these
tiny smooth pink ones like babies' fingernails –
strewn all over her bedside table. The Jiffy bag was

a giveaway. Torn open. Small slanty handwriting.

"Did Dunkin Donuts send these?" I say.

"No," says Isabel going all pink.

She's useless at lying. I can read her like a book.

"We've been e-mailing," she says.

"Since when?" I say.

"About a week," she says.

Turns out they've been in touch every day for a week. Late night messages.

How cosy!

"He makes me laugh," she says.

"So how come you didn't say?" I ask. I'm trying not to feel too hurt she kept it secret. She doesn't really give me an answer to that one.

"What's he like?" I say. "What sort of stuff does he write? Or is it private?"

She blushes again.

"Oh my God, he doesn't write filth does he?"

"*No!*" she says. "Of course not!" She picks up a long blue shell and starts fiddling with it. I look at her quizzically, knowing that she'll crack. And she does. She shows me all the stuff in her mail box. His messages to her and hers back to him.

"This guy is *nice!*" I say. She smiles.

"So why are you going on a date with hedgehog hair?" I say.

"It's not a *date*," she says, shutting down the

computer. I'm looking at her like I don't believe her for a minute.

"Honest!" she says.

Why do I get the feeling she's lying?

Act II Scene x

Isabel sits on her bed, fiddling with shells. Books and bits of homework and discarded clothes are scattered about the floor. She is listening to Nina Simone.

ISABEL:

Duncan sent me some shells. They came in a Jiffy bag with a handwritten note.

Dear Miranda

Here are some shells for your hair. Isabel told me you needed them. I collected them on Traigh Mor (which is Gaelic for "big beach"). Traigh Mor is the biggest beach on Rimsay. Two miles of creamy white sand and huge dunes – home to thousands of rabbits, which Boris (my dog) likes chasing! I am – right at this moment – writing an essay about *The Tempest*. Here is the title question: " '*I do forgive thee, unnatural as thou art . . .*' Consider Prospero's forgiveness of his enemies. How important is it to the play as a whole?" If you have any ideas I would be very grateful!

Better go now

Love, Duncan

PS Keep away from Ferdinand. I hear he's bad news!

I sent Duncan an e-mail after Macy had left.

Dear Duncan

Thanx for the lovely shells. Miranda really liked them! Your description of the beach sounded like a holiday brochure. The beach beside our cottage (in Ardnamurchan) had big dunes – and loads of rabbits too. But it rained six days out of seven. Were we unlucky or is that normal for Scotland?

So how is your essay coming along? I asked Miranda what she thought of her father forgiving Uncle Antonio and she said she was glad because it meant she could get off the island, back to sunny Italy and wash her hair again! I think secretly she was sad to leave all the sand and shells behind.

Prospero forgives Antonio without Antonio – or any of the others – ever saying sorry. I reckon that's a bit over the top, personally. But if someone says sorry, maybe that's different.

While we're on the subject, do you mind if I ask you a question? Jamie (that's the former-love-of-my-life) now says he's sorry he dumped me. Macy says I should tell him to sit and spin. She says no second chance – once a git, always a git. But I'm not so sure. I think people can change. To forgive or not to forgive? *That* is the question!

So, how are the Posh Porpoises doing? Is Ned any better at keeping in time? What do you sound like? Do you write your own songs?

Sorry ... this is turning into twenty questions!!! Time to get down to some homework. Thanks again for the fab shells. Now I've just got to work out how to fix them in my (sorry Miranda's) hair.

Love, Isabel

I hadn't put "Love, Isabel" before, but he'd put "Love, Duncan" in his letter so I just did. I typed an X after my name but then I changed my mind and deleted it. I thought for a moment and then I added a PS:

PS You know you said *The Tempest* was about love at first sight ... Do you *believe* in love at first sight?

Then I clicked "*Send.*"

Act III Scene i

Enter Isabel, fresh out of the shower and wrapped in a blue and white bath towel. She is cleaning her teeth.

ISABEL:

The gang going to the pictures turned out to be just me and Jamie. Phil forgot to come, Natalie had to babysit and Jamie's friend Ig said he was too skint to go out. So low key nite out with loads of mates ended up as cosy date for two, after all.

Jamie called for me. I was upstairs trying to get my hair to look half-decent. It had been looking lank so I'd washed it, but then it had gone all static and frizzy. I'd run out of wax so the best chance I had of presentable hair was Mum's mousse, which smells like cheap aftershave. I bet Miranda never had these problems.

Mum gave Jamie a coffee, and when I came downstairs he was perched on a kitchen stool with his hand in the cookie tin, chatting to Mum – just like old times. He looked great – hoodie and carpenter pants. Pete sauntered in from his home-office and made a typically sarcastic comment, "You could have washed your trousers, Jamie!" Jamie laughed. That was all Pete said. Before Jamie came, I'd wondered if they'd give him a hard time. It was the first time Mum and Pete had seen him since we split up and he hadn't exactly been flavour of the month in our house over the summer. But they were both polite to him. Polite and friendly, as if nothing bad had happened. Maybe they'd forgiven him. And if they had, why shouldn't I?

"How's Alice?" Jamie asked.

"Fine," Mum said. "She's coming home tomorrow. Just for the weekend."

I was glad Alice wasn't there a day early. I'm not sure I'd have trusted *her* to forgive Jamie. She'd be more likely to slap his face!

The evening was uneventful. We caught a bus to the cinema. The film wasn't great. Too much shooting and women in leather pants. I think Jamie enjoyed it. But then, he likes Britney! We caught a bus home again. At the cinema, Jamie didn't touch me – apart from when he accidentally brushed against me as we sat down – and I didn't touch *him*. We were cool. We just chatted, like friends. Just friends. But on the way home we held hands. It seemed like a natural thing to do. Comfortable.

I checked my mail box before I went to bed. There was a yellow envelope – one message unread.

Dear Isabel

Thank you for using our on-line agony aunt service. Here are some answers to your questions – in order of unimportance.

1. Yes, we have the *Beano* on Rimsay, but I stopped reading it when I was eight.

2. No, you weren't unlucky. One dry day in seven is pretty good going for Scotland!

3. The Posh Porpoises are sounding better than ever since Ned resigned as drummer and agreed to be our manager/roadie. We even managed to find a new drummer – Ned's cousin Kate – who, it turns out, is a natural born rhythm chick.

4. We sound like a cross between Travis, Ash, Oasis and Iron Maiden. Think Badly Drawn Boy without the woolly hat!

5. We mostly do cover versions but one or two of our songs are mine, and we do a wild heavy rock version of the Britney classic *Oops, I Did it Again!*

6. I think love at first sight is highly likely – especially for crazy island dwellers, starved of male (or indeed female) company.

7. I think forgiveness is as vital as air. Without it love dies.

8. I think only *you* can decide whether you want to give Jamie-the-git a second chance.

However, if you decide to go for it, tell him from me if he messes you about again I'll beat the crap out of him.

9. Whatever you decide – respect yourself.

10. And finally, those shells . . . You're asking the wrong guy here, but Superglue should do the trick.

Not twenty questions, only ten.

Hope you're well. I borrowed a Dido album from Kate (the rhythm chick). I like it – though it's a little too mellow for my taste. I lost the will to live after the first five tracks! But I like the song called *Isobel* (except she's spelt it wrong!)

Love Duncan x

I replied – briefly, because it was late.

Dear Duncan

Thanks for your comprehensive e-agony aunt service. I will recommend it to all my friends!

I also like the Dido song *Isobel* though I agree it's a little depressing! Unlike the Posh Porpoises – who sound *wicked*!

As if I havn't asked enough questions already here's another . . .

What's it like on your island? I feel like I

**need to know more about islands to really get
into Miranda's character.**

    Love Isabel x

Act III Scene ii

Lights up on the drama studio. Isabel sits on a chair, eating her lunch.

ISABEL:

The photo shoot was hilarious. Mr Kempe needed pictures of Prospero (Sebastian), Antonio (Chloe Stretton), Alonso the King (Rosie Mason) and Gonzalo the kind old courtier (Phil Colvin). He didn't need me, but I went along for the laugh. It was Friday lunchtime. I was eating an apple and a Fruit Corner yogurt.

Mr Kempe had rigged a blue sheet on the studio wall as a back drop. No one had proper costumes yet but Ms Redman had brought along some token bits and pieces for atmosphere.

Sebastian put on this long leather coat – Luftwaffe style – and a wide-brimmed hat with a satin band round it. He stood there, looking grand and pompous – Prospero, the rightful Duke of Milan.

"Brilliant," said Mr Kempe, and the camera flashed twice.

"Now, Antonio," Ms Redman said. "We need two shots of you, Chloe. In the first one I want you smiling." Chloe turned up the collar of her leather jacket and did a big cheesy smile.

"Great stuff," said Mr Kempe. "Stay there, I'll take a few." The camera flashed twice more.

"Now you need to put on Sebastian's hat and coat," Ms Redman said. "*You're* the Duke of Milan now. You've overthrown Prospero."

"Mine!" said Chloe darkly, snatching the hat off Sebastian's head.

Next was Rosie Mason – the King of Naples – in a Cinderella crown we found in the props cupboard and a velvet cloak the colour of dried blood.

"Look shifty," Ms Redman said . . .

"And finally, Gonzalo," said Mr Kempe.

Phil Colvin took Rosie's place against the blue sheet.

"You need to look old and kind," Ms Redman said.

We found him a bowler hat.

"Laurel and Hardy!" Phil said with a grin.

"Put your specs on maybe?" Ms Redman said, and Phil took his glasses out of his pocket. They looked a bit trendy.

"You don't look old enough," said Mr Kempe.

"Hang on a minute," Phil said, and he disappeared out through the studio door.

Sebastian started practising his lines about being dumped on a dodgy ship: "*There they hoist us to cry to th'sea that roared to us, to sigh to th'winds, whose pity sighing back again did us but loving wrong . . ."*

"*Alack what trouble was I then to you!*" I said, hearing my cue line.

"*O, a cherubin thou wast that did preserve me . . .*" Sebastian replied. He gave me a fond smile and then he said, "*How* old is Miranda when they leave Italy?"

"Three," I said.

"Could we have a slide of Miranda then, aged three, to complete the set?" he said.

"What a good idea," Ms Redman said. "Have you got a photo of you at that age, Isabel?"

"Probably," I said. Mum's got book-loads of photos of us. Most of them deeply embarassing! "I'll have a look at the weekend," I said.

"Preferably looking cherubic," said Sebastian.

"Don't I always?" I said.

Phil came back wearing Mr Cheesman's glasses. Mr Cheesman teaches Maths and he's ancient and wrinkly. His glasses are little gold hoops, like Captain Mainwaring off *Dad's Army*.

"Brilliant!" said Ms Redman.

"Smile please," said Mr Kempe . . .

The last photograph was the best. Ms Redman wanted all four of them, plus Sebastian the king's brother (Jude Lomax), and the courtiers who get shipwrecked with them – Adrian (Sara Bottomley) and Francisco (Jenny Murphy) – all on one photo together. And she wanted them *wet*! *Soaking* wet!

"You're washed up on the shores of Prospero's island," she said.

"Can I tip a bucket of water over them?" Sebastian said, with glee.

"No, it'll make the floor too slippery. I've got Year Sevens in here after lunch!" Ms Redman said with a laugh. "Can you go to the loos and wet your hair and faces?" she asked and off they all went.

They came back drenched. Chloe looked like she'd been in the shower. "I hope you didn't drip all over the corridors, or I'll be in trouble," Ms Redman said, grinning at Mr Kempe.

"OK, quick now," Mr Kempe said. "Huddle together and look bewildered." They huddled convincingly. "Brilliant," he said. The camera flashed three times and then the bell rang for afternoon school.

Act III Scene iii

*Lights up on Isabel and Macy with carrier bags
full of shopping.*

ISABEL:

Macy and I have a free period directly after lunch
on Fridays. Doe had given us permission to go
off-site to cruise second-hand shops looking for
costumes. "See what you can find – shirts, T-shirts,
trousers, jackets. Go for cotton and linen rather
than nylon, so we can dye stuff easily," Doe said.
She gave us forty quid – four crisp tenners. Macy
pocketed the cash.

"We *could* just go for a late lunch at La Viva,"
she said, as we walked out through the school
gates. "And say we were mugged!" It was an
appealing thought. I was still hungry after my apple
and yogurt. Sit me in front of grilled ciabatta with
mozzarella and roasted peppers, and a slice of
whisky marmalade cake and my willpower would
dissolve away to nothing!

"Don't tempt me," I answered.

In Oxfam we found a long denim coat (£5.00) and
some white jeans (£1.99). The jeans had a black ink

stain on the knee, which is why they were so cheap.

"These'll dye brilliantly," Macy said, taking the hanger off the rail. In Help the Aged, Macy spotted a linen skirt (£3.50), and I found some white size five canvas shoes (£2) and a blue silk scarf (99p). At the Quit Smoking shop we got five T-shirts, nonedescript colours, for a fiver.

"Bargain!" said Macy, in a daft cockney accent.

"Definitely!" I said, stuffing them into a bag.

But best of all was the Imperial Cancer Research Fund shop – matching white cheesecloth skirt and top, hippy style (£4.50 the set), three pairs of jeans – size twelve, size sixteen and men's extra large (£2 each), a velvet waistcoat, silvery grey (£3), a long grey old lady's mac (£2) and a pair of dark blue velvet curtains (£4.50).

"Prospero's cloak," I said.

"We've got one pound fifty-two left," Macy said, counting out the coins in her pocket. We were outside Boots.

"God, that didn't go far!" I said.

"We've got loads," said Macy, holding up the bags she was carrying. "My arms are dropping off."

She was right. We had six carrier bags full.

"One pound fifty-two," Macy said again. "That'll buy one cappuccino and a cherry flapjack at Coffee Republic. We can share them."

I laughed. "Nice try," I said, "but I need a mirror."

"What for?" Macy said.

"Wait and see," I said.

We went to Wilkinsons. I found a mirror for £1.99 with a disgusting green frame.

"Gross frame," Macy said.

"I don't need the frame," I said. "Just the mirror."

"You're forty-seven pence short," Macy said. I handed her a fifty-pence piece from my purse. We were queueing at the check-out when my phone bleeped.

"Text message!" Macy announced to the whole store. It was Jamie: "*Great 2 c u last nite. C u at rehearsal. Luv J xxx*".

"Who's it from?" Macy said. She was handing over the money to the checkout girl.

"Mum," I lied. "Reminding me about something."

"Reminding you about what?" Macy said.

"Three pence change," the checkout girl said.

"Some shopping I said I'd get," I answered, walking towards the exit.

"What shopping?" Macy said. There was a big display of discount toilet rolls in the shop doorway.

"Toilet rolls!" I said suddenly. "We've run out."

"Well buy some then," Macy said. "Look! They're on special offer!"

"I'll get some on the way home," I said. Macy looked unconvinced. She knew I was bluffing. She probably guessed it was Jamie. I just didn't want her giving me advice. Especially when she loathes him so much.

The rehearsal after school was the pageant scene – the one where all the godesses and nymphs bless Miranda and Ferdinand with long life and happiness. The maypole dance was working really well now, except that Sara Bottomley kept getting her ribbon tangled up. Kirsty Baker had learnt all her lines. "You were really good," I said to her after the scene was over. I meant it. She looked pleased.

"Thanks," she said gratefully.

Chloe Stretton was painting some flats in a corner of the studio – triangular panels, four of them, free-standing, about three metres tall. They looked a bit like sails. Chloe had made frames out of wood and stretched coarse white fabric across them, held on to the frames with tacks. Now she was painting blue and grey abstract designs on them.

At the rehearsal, Ms Redman had marked out the acting space with masking tape, so we got more of an idea of how it will feel. We're performing the play in the studio, using floor level as the stage. The audience will sit on three sides on raised seating, so they'll be higher than us. At the back of the stage will be a screen wall (for the slides) and Chloe's flats, arranged to create entrances and exits. Just left of centre stage will be a rostra construction – wrapped in fabric to look like rocks – that we can sit or stand on, or go inside. Caliban's going to use it for his cave (Ms Redman changed her mind about the blanket idea) and Jamie and I will sit inside it when we play chess. There'll be a curtain across the front that Prospero can draw back.

"Think of the audience as the sea," Ms Redman said, "lapping at the edges of the shore."

I suggested putting sand on the floor but Doe said that would be too complicated and we might slip.

"What about debris, like you find on a beach?" Macy said.

"Like what?" Doe said.

"Seaweed?" said Macy.

"Might be a bit difficult to get hold of," Doe said.

Macy looked at me and winked. I knew what she was thinking.

Act III Scene iv

Lights up on Isabel, Hoovering her room. She switches off the Hoover and starts sorting the pile of clothes, books and papers that is heaped on her bed.

ISABEL:

I'd just finished writing my rehearsal diary when Mum and Alice arrived home from the station. Alice looked great. She had a new haircut and had gone blonde. Blonder than normal, anyway. She dumped her bag in the hall and gave me a hug. "Hi, little Iz," she said affectionately. "How's the play going?"

"Great," I said. "How's uni?"

"Groovy," said Alice. She flung her coat on the bannisters. Pete came into the hallway and gave Al a hug.

"Term going well?" he said.

"Yep," said Alice.

"Spent all your money?" Pete said.

"Tell me about it!" said Al.

"Tea'll be about half an hour," said Mum, banging cupboards in the kitchen.

Al took her stuff up to her room and flopped down on the bed. "I'm exhausted," she said, yawning dramatically. "The train was packed and I had to stand all the way to York." I sat down on her bed. "So what's new?" she said, rolling on to her side and propping herself on her elbow.

I told her about the play, and Doe and Mr Kempe (Macy's convinced they're an item!), and our charity shop trawl, and Chloe Stretton's party. I didn't tell her about going to the pictures with Jamie. But I *did* tell her about the message in a bottle.

"You're kidding!" she squealed. "Someone actually *found* it!"

"Yeah," I said. "Amazing isn't it?" For all I'd downplayed it when it actually happened – when Macy was going on about Duncan's letter being miraculous – it *was* pretty amazing that the note had survived all that time and travelled all that way.

I told Al about Duncan. That he'd found her note on the beach. That he'd written to me from his island. I didn't tell her how many times he'd written – or how many messages I'd sent to him.

"What's he like?" she said, sitting up on the bed.

"He seems OK," I said, casually.

"Tea's ready," Mum shouted.

Mum had made vegetarian lasagne and salad.

"Mmmm! Real food," said Alice. "Thanks Mum."

We were halfway through eating it, and Alice was telling us about the girls in her flat and all their filthy habits, and the mad Irish landlady, and some bloke in her Maths group who used to live next door to David Beckham, when suddenly she said, "Isn't it incredible about Izzy's message?"

"What message?" said Mum. I hadn't told Mum and Pete about Duncan. I wasn't being deliberately secretive. I just hadn't wanted to make a fuss about it. About him.

Alice told them the lot. How we'd written the note on the beach at Ardnamurchan. How she'd put it in the Bacardi Breezer bottle. How I'd paddled out and thrown it in the sea. How some guy called Duncan had found it and written me a letter.

"So *that's* the mystery Scottish postmark," said Pete. "I was dying to ask about that but Mum told me not to be nosy!"

"Fancy you not telling us," Mum said, looking surprised.

"Mysterious Isabel," said Al, teasing me.

Pete got down from the table and rummaged in the cupboard beside the hi-fi system.

"*Now* what's he up to?" said Mum, stabbing a cherry tomato with her fork. Pete's got a huge collection of vinyl – tatty old albums from the seventies and eighties. Dinosaur Rock, Al calls it.

"Ta-da!" said Pete, pulling out a battered album

sleeve. He took the record out of the sleeve and put it on the turntable. Then he lifted the needle, carefully, into the middle of it. It made a scratchy, hissing sound. "Oops, wrong track," he said. He tried again. It was The Police. I recognized it from the greatest hits tape he plays all the time in the car. "*Message in a bottle!*" he said.

Sting's voice blared out: "*I hope that someone gets my, I hope that someone gets my mess-age in a bott-le!*"

"Cheers, Pete," I said with a smile.

I checked my e-mail after tea. "*There are no new messages*" it said. I felt a stab of disappointment that took me by surprise. Alice had been planning to go out and catch up with her mates, but she was so tired she stayed in. I was tired too. We crashed on the sofa and watched *ER*. Jamie sent me a text message: "*How r u?*" Then a row of hearts and a row of smiley faces. Mum had told Alice about Jamie coming round last night.

"That's not from Ego-boy is it?" Al said, when she heard my phone beep.

" 'Fraid so," I said. She'd find out sooner or later – if we started seeing each other again. If . . .

"You're mad," she said.

I looked at her and went bog-eyed.

"Sad girl," Al said, shaking her head.

Mum made me have an early night. She said I

looked pasty. I couldn't resist checking my mail again before I got into bed. Just in case. *"Checking for mail . . . Receiving mail . . . One message unread:"*

Dear Isabel

Hi! You asked me about my island so I'll try and describe it. Here goes . . .

Rimsay is nine kilometres long and five kilometres wide. It is west of Mull and south-west of Skye. There is one small town – Seabay – on the south side of the island, and three smaller settlements – Northton, Scarpa and Kerravore. Seabay has four shops, two hotels, a café, a community hall and three churches. There is a road that goes right round the island in a loop and buses run four times a day. A car ferry comes from Oban on Sundays, Tuesdays and Thursdays – unless the sea's too rough for it to dock at the pier (in which case we all run out of bread and fresh milk!). There's also an airport (the landing strip's on the beach!) with flights from Glasgow twice a week, weather permitting. There's one secondary school, Seabay Community High School, which has fifty-eight pupils (including me). There's a fish processing plant near Northton (look out for the smell on a hot day!), a fudge factory (Taste of the Hebrides Quality Confectionery) at

Seabay, and a whisky distillery (free dram with every guided tour) at Kerravore. Visitors might like to visit the Museum of Island Life (open Tuesdays and Fridays – summer season only) situated in the building adjacent to Seabay Island Centre! Blah blah blah . . . that's the official stuff.

But what's it *really* like?

Well, it's incredibly beautiful – in a wild, unspoilt, open-to-the-elements, no-frills sort of way! There are the beaches for starters. It's like the Bahamas, without the palm trees (no trees at all in fact – too windy!), *and* without the sun! Then there's the machair (pronounced mack-er) which is meadowland beside the shore. The Hebrides are famous for it – apparently! In spring it's covered with wild flowers. Our house faces east and there's nothing but machair from us to the shore. When it's warm, my granddad likes to sit out the front and just stare at the flowers. He calls them "God's jewels."

There are lots of cows and sheep – more sheep than people, in fact. The sheep wander everywhere and the cows crap on the beach!

Then there's the wildlife . . . We have Golden Eagles (you can see *them* over the hill behind Kerravore). Porpoises you know about, and lots of seals. On the rocks at the far end of Traigh Mor you can hear the seals singing in the evening. Sometimes I ride there on my bike to listen to them. On the clifftop west of here there's a blow hole that they call the Kelpie's Breath. When the tide's coming in, the waves spurt up through a hole in the rocks, like a fountain. It makes a fantastic noise like a giant champagne cork popping. And then there are the Singing Sands – up on the north side, where the best scallops are. If you lie on the beach with your ear to the ground you can hear the sand singing. Honest, you can! My granny used to say it was drowned men's souls wailing on the seabed.

The sea is pretty important to islanders. It's everywhere you look and its mood is forever changing. Sometimes it's as flat as glass. Then it can be like a raging beast, battering the shore. It washes things up all the time – driftwood, rubbish, dead whales, letters from crazy English girls! Island people love the sea, but they fear it too. It gives and it takes away. My cousin Joe drowned in a fishing accident when he was sixteen. Everyone knows *someone* who's died in the sea.

Another thing about islands – am I going on too much? – is that everyone knows your business. It's a close-knit community, which is nice in a way I suppose. But there's no escape! And there's no one new, which can get monotonous. (Miranda would know all about *that*! "*O brave new world that has such people in it!!!*") There's the odd tourist, but most of them are American and old. Mum does bed and breakfast in the summer, so our house gets invaded by men in tartan caps and Pringle sweaters! But it pays the bills. Everyone on Rimsay is trying to scratch a living. Dad's got three jobs. He drives the post bus, services people's boats and catches lobsters and fish. Mum's got three jobs too. She's a home care worker – making meals for old people – and she works in the café, and she does B&B. On top of that, she looks after my granddad who's got Alzheimer's disease. No wonder people on Rimsay drink a lot of whisky!

Oh, and they're mostly mad too. Mad, religious and deeply superstitious. There are all these crazy island stories about magic and fairy folk and seals with legs that walk out of the sea and drink your cows' milk in the dead of night! And you thought *The Tempest* was weird!

Yes, there's definitely something strange about islands. People go mad from endless wind and too much sky!

So that's us – the loony folk of Rimsay! I hope this helps you understand Miranda, and that you won't stop writing to me now you know I'm bonkers!

Cheers, Isabel. Love Duncan x

So much for my early night. I closed down the computer and went to bed, where I dreamt of turquoise sea and singing seals.

Act III Scene v

Enter Isabel in ballet tights and a leotard. She is stretching at the bar.

ISABEL:

It was good to be back at dance. I warmed up, going through each position, doing pliés and—

"How's *The Tempest* going?" Siobhan said, pulling her cardigan off over her head.

"It's coming together," I said. "A lot of people don't know their lines, though."

Chloe and Rosie and Phil Colvin were still using their books at rehearsals. Doe had given them this weekend to get word-perfect. "I don't want to see *any* scripts at rehearsals next week!" she'd said on Friday. "And we're not having a prompt! Get those words *up here*." She'd tapped her forehead as she said that and her hair had fallen across her face.

"It's less than two weeks now till your first night, isn't it?" Siobhan said, putting her toe on to the bar.

It was. It was under a fortnight. First nights always make me *so* nervous. I'm a jibbering wreck – in and out of the loo! I felt a quick spasm of terror at the thought of it. "Nerves are good," Reggie Clarke used to say. "They keep you on your toes." On my toes? On the toilet more like!

After my jazz class, I got changed and went for the bus to singing. Someone had spilt a bag of chips at the bus stop and a flock of pigeons were devouring them. *"How many goodly creatures are there here?"* I said to them. *"How beauteous mankind is! O brave new world that has such pigeons in't!"* And Duncan's worried that *he's* mad!

My bus came round the corner with a hiss of brakes, and the pigeons scattered, taking beakfuls of chips with them.

I peeled a satsuma on the bus and ate it slowly – a segment for every character in the play. One for Prospero, one for Antonio, one for Ariel, one for Trinculo, one for Miranda, one for Ferdinand . . .

The bus stopped at the lights beside Jamie's house. I looked to the right, instinctively. His curtains were open. His bed was unmade. My eyes searched the room for a glimpse of Jamie. He wasn't there. As the bus pulled away I felt a pang of disappointment. Look out, Isabel . . . you're slipping!

Mr O'Leary was wearing a spotted bow tie. "You're looking very lovely today, Isabel," he said, spinning round on his stool.

I put my bag on the floor and took off my shoes. Mr O'Leary reckons people sing better in bare feet.

"And how is the voice?" he said, beaming at me.

My voice was a bit ropey. "You *are* taking care to warm up the voice before rehearsals, aren't you?" he said. "Plenty of diaphragm breathing so you don't strain the vocal chords." He looked at me as if my vocal chords were a matter of life and death. Perhaps they are! After all, what's an actor without a voice?

We sang some scales and some arpeggios and then I sang my breakfast: "Coffee and toast with peanut butter."

"Was it smooth or crun-chy?" he replied, in an answering phrase.

"It (. . . two, three . . .) was crun-chy!" I sang, like an echo. Did all singing teachers do such mad stuff? Macy goes to a woman called Milly who's a jazz singer. I bet *she* doesn't make her sing about peanut butter.

After the musical discussion about my breakfast, I sang my Mozart aria. I bet he could tell I hadn't practised it since the last lesson. The high note sounded like I was being strangled.

"I think it's time for a new piece," he said, at the end of it. "Let's have a change . . . Something a bit lighter . . ."

He opened a document wallet and took out the

sheet music for *Love Changes Everything* by Andrew Lloyd Webber. I had to sight-sing it, which was easy because I know it anyway. Dad took me to see *Aspects of Love* at the London Palladium for my tenth birthday. I sang the songs for weeks afterwards in the bathroom mirror, with a bottle of shampoo for my microphone. (Al's right when she says I'm a sad girl!) I sang *Love Changes Everything* enthusiastically – *con brio* (with brightness) – and Mr O'Leary joined in, doing harmonies. It's such a cheesy song but it made me feel absurdly happy. Sun was streaming in through the window. The carpet was warm under my bare feet. Love did change everything. And forgiveness is as vital as air.

My phone bleeped while I was singing the song a second time. I ignored it because Mr O'Leary thinks phones are "wretched things". But as I was walking down his garden path after my lesson, I checked it. *"One new message"*: *"Meet u in town? At the tulip? 1pm? Luv J"*.

It was Jamie. I felt a quick surge of pleasure.

"Reply?" my phone asked. I looked at my watch. It was twelve thirty-five. I wouldn't have time to go home and make it for one. Pete was waiting in the car.

"Pete, would you mind dropping me in the city centre instead of going home? I'm meeting someone . . ."

Pete looked at the clock on the dashboard. "The traffic will be bad, there's a match at Old Trafford," he said.

"Won't we miss it, going this early?" I said, hopefully.

"Just about," Pete said. "What about your lunch?"

"I'll get something in town," I said. Pete looked reluctant. Maybe I should just text Jamie and say not to bother. Why do I want to see him so much anyway? Love changes everything . . . Suddenly I remembered I had a trump card. "I need to get Mum a present," I said. "For tomorrow . . ." Tomorrow was Mum's birthday. She was forty-five.

"Go on then," Pete said.

"Cheers Pete," I said.

I pressed "*Reply*" and sent a message to Jamie. "*Tulip is fine. Can we make it one-fifteen? CU Iz*".

Then I flipped down the sun flap above the passenger seat and looked in the mirror. What a mess! Perhaps I should have gone home first after all. My hair looked awful.

"Bad hair day!" I said to Pete, who smiled sympathetically. My fringe was flopping over my eyes. I was desperate to get it cut.

"Wait till after the play," Macy had said. "Or it will be too short to plait." We'd decided what to do with the shells. Macy was going to plait braids in my hair and then sew the shells into the plaits with cotton.

"You'll have to leave it in for the three days though," she had said, " 'cos it will take ages to do." Imagine, not washing your hair for *three* days! (*Four*, if I did it for the dress rehearsal.)

Pete dropped me on Deansgate outside Habitat. It was five to one. I just had time to get to the Body Shop to discreetly apply some make-up at the testers bar. My hair would have to do. Anyway, Jamie likes it (or used to like it!) when my fringe hangs across my eyes. He thinks it's sexy. I pouted into the mirror and applied some lipstick to my mouth.

"You're supposed to test it on the back of your hand," said someone behind me. I jumped and turned round. It was Sara Bottomley. She was spraying perfume on her wrists.

"Ssh!" I said, putting a finger to my freshly-glistening lips.

I unscrewed the top off an eye-pencil (cappuccino – how appropriate!) and drew a smudgy line under my lashes. Then I looked at myself in the mirror. That was better. There's nothing like a lick of paint!

On my way out, a sales assistant tried to get me to sample a tub of hazelnut body butter. "It isn't tested on animals," she said, "and it's made from fairly-traded cocoa butter." It smelt like chocolate spread.

"Thanks," I said, "but I'm in a bit of a hurry."

Jamie was waiting for me when I arrived. The tulip is a concrete fountain – tulip-shaped (you don't say!) – in St Ann's square. Jamie was sitting on a bench beside it. A busker with a violin and a yellow dog was playing Irish jigs in the doorway of the Disney store. The music made me want to dance.

"Hi," said Jamie, touching my arm. He looked gorgeous.

"Thanks for coming," he said. As he smiled, the edges of his mouth turned up ever so slightly.

"What did you want to do?" I said. My palms felt prickly. I was nervous. Why was I nervous?

"Whatever," said Jamie, with a shrug.

"I need to get a birthday present for Mum," I said. "Do you mind if I do that first?"

"Fine," Jamie said. He was looking at me as if *anything* I suggested would be fine. As if he'd follow me to the moon.

We went to Wax Lyrical. I bought Mum an Essential Pampering kit – soap, shampoo, moisturizer, lip balm, a flannel and a loofah, all in a clear plastic bucket. It was £12.49, which was a rip-off but I reckoned she'd like it.

"Shall I get 'Revitalizing' or 'Mellow'?" I asked Jamie.

"Mellow, definitely," Jamie said. His voice sent a

shiver down the back of my neck. Had he always been that sexy?

They put Mum's present in a purple carrier bag. I took it and went back out into the square.

"Do you want to get lunch?" Jamie said.

"I'm skint now," I said. Mum's present had cleaned me out. My allowance wasn't due till next week.

"I've got loads-a-money," said Jamie, in a silly voice.

"Did you sleep at your dad's last night?" I said. He nodded.

Jamie's dad lives on the other side of Manchester. He goes there every other Friday night (used to anyway). His dad's got a new wife and a baby and three stepkids – so he hasn't really got time for Jamie. But he always gives him lots of cash.

"Will he come and see the play?" I said.

"I doubt it," Jamie said. A look flashed across his face. I've seen the look before. It's a lost boy sort of look – fragile, easy to hurt, bordering on pathetic.

I had a strong desire to kiss him and make it all better but I didn't want to be over the top, so instead I said, "Let's spend your money, then!"

We went to Starbucks. I had a toasted pannini with olives and roasted peppers, and a white chocolate mocha. Jamie told me a funny story about his dad's baby peeing into a box full of lego. I told him about Alice's flatmate cutting her toenails into Alice's favourite cup. When we left the café, Jamie held my hand. I laced my fingers into his. The violinist with the yellow dog had moved on. Now a girl in leather was playing *Summertime* on a saxophone. The music slid lazily across the square. In the corner by St Ann's church a barrow was selling flowers. Jamie stopped and pulled out his wallet. He bought a rose – a yellow one because they didn't have any red ones – and gave it to me. I put it between my teeth like a Flamenco dancer.

"Olé!" he said, and I hugged him.

We moseyed round the shops a bit. We went in Gap and Kookai and the Virgin V-shop. Then we went into Jake's, which is my favourite shoe shop. Jamie knows what I'm like about shoes. There were these wicked blue satin mules with kitten heels and a pointed toe. They were covered in sequins and embroidery. I picked one up and turned it over. A sticker on the sole said £49.99.

"Bit steep," I said.

We walked passed the kids' section. There was a tiny weeny pair of patent leather Kickers boots – post-box red – baby size.

"Cute," said Jamie. (Jamie loves babies. He says he wants six!)

We walked along King Street. Outside Vidal Sasson was a blackboard. "Models wanted for free haircuts – Thursday 9pm," it said.

"I'm desperate for a haircut," I said.

"Why?" said Jamie. "Your hair's lovely. Especially this bit . . ." He took hold of a hank of my fringe – the bit that was trailing in my eyes – and fiddled with it. (See!) We were facing each other, on the pavement outside Monsoon. Jamie let go of my hair and ran his finger down my cheek. I caught a glimpse of us in the shop window. We looked good together.

We caught a Number 87 bus from Cross Street and rode on the top deck, at the front. Jamie folded his arm around my shoulders and I snuggled up close. It felt as natural as breathing. I'd forgiven him. I knew that for certain. And I was sliding. There was no way back. We were becoming a couple again. And it felt fantastic!

"Let's get off a stop early and walk through the park," Jamie said.

It was sunny. We walked under coppery trees and tramped through piles of crunchy leaves.

"I love autumn," I said.

"I love *you*," Jamie said. I believed him. He was looking at me with big brown eyes. He kissed me. I kissed him back. Warm soft mouths that knew each other's shape. It was like our first kiss all over again. My insides turned to liquid – pools of golden honey.

A boy hurtled past us on a skateboard. Jamie pushed my hair out of my eyes.

"I love you too," I said. There. I'd said it. There was no going back.

"Happy?" Jamie said. I nodded blissfully.

Act III Scene vi

Isabel enters and sits on her bed. She threads a needle and ties a knot in the end of the navy blue thread.

ISABEL:

Mum's birthday was treats all the way. First we took her tea and prezzies in bed. Mum's a real "mornings" person. She was all perky and smiley, sitting propped up in bed with her tea tray. Pete was grunting from under the covers. Al and I clambered in bed with them – like we used to when we were little.

Mum was wearing an old T-shirt with Tweetie-Pie on the front. I gave her the "Pampering Kit". She really liked it. She took the lid off and inhaled the smell. "Yum," she said. "Mell-ow," and she kissed my cheek.

I remembered the way Jamie had said "mellow" in the shop and smiled to myself. I was still glowing from yesterday – glowing like a ripe peach!

Alice's present was a Jamie Oliver cookbook. "Happy dayth!" Al said with an exaggerated lisp.

"Look, Pete," said Mum.

"Lovely," said Pete, without opening his eyes. He

was lying with his face buried in the pillow. Without lifting his head, he reached out from under the covers and groped about on the floor under the bed. "Happy birthday," he said, groggily, pulling out a parcel wrapped in pink hearts, and a huge card.

"Oh, bless!" said Alice. Pete and Alice are really close. She was ten when he came on the scene. I was only seven. Mum was a mess. Al was the big sister, looking after Mum and holding it all together. I think she was eternally grateful that Pete made Mum smile again. Mr Bright – putting the sunshine back.

Pete's present was a Robbie Williams CD and some silver earrings.

"Thank you," Mum said, kissing the bald patch on the top of Pete's head.

After breakfast, Mum had a long, lazy bath while Al and I made lunch. We were pretty ambitious – thanks to Alice. Lamb chops marinated in garlic, honey and ginger. New potatoes roasted in their skins (with sea salt and olive oil), and ratatouille. I was chief chopper: onions, aubergines, courgettes, mushrooms, parsley – you name it, I can chop it!

"Do you need any help?" Pete said. He was sprawled on the sofa reading the Sunday papers.

"No, everything's under control," said Al. "But you could go and buy some wine – and some ice cream, maybe. Get some Ben and Jerry's – Mum loves that . . ."

"What flavour?" Pete said.

"Fudge Brownie," said Alice.

"Full Vermonty!" I said.

"I'll get both," said Pete.

We'd just licked out the last dribbles of ice cream from the tub when Mum's friend Jan arrived to give her a birthday foot massage. "More pampering," said Mum, smiling. They went off into the sitting-room and Pete took them coffee and After Eight mints.

I went upstairs. My room was a mess. There were clothes all over the floor. I picked up the top I'd been wearing yesterday. It smelt of Jamie. I pressed my face into it.

I had English homework – a poetry question about Andrew Marvell's *To His Coy Mistress*. I switched on the computer. Since I still hadn't replied to Duncan's epic message, I went online and wrote:

Dear Duncan

Thanks for your amazing description of your island. It sounds like paradise – you must really love it. I'd love to hear the seals singing. What does it sound like? There I go again! Asking questions! Little Miss Nosey!

I'm sure you're not mad. You sound pretty sane to me – but then what would *I* know about it?

Today is my mum's birthday. Alice (my sister) is home from uni for the weekend. It totally freaked her out when I told her you found our (or rather *her*) message. She wants to meet you!

Well, must fly. I've masses of homework and Prospero's cloak to make too.

Take care, love Isabel

PS Yet more questions . . . What kind of things wash up on the shore? (Apart from dead whales and messages in bottles!)

It was a bit skimpy – considering he'd written me a whole essay. But it would have to do. I was halfway through my English homework when a message came back.

Dear Busy Izzy

Wood, blue nylon rope, fishing net (acres of it), fishing floats, shampoo bottles – plastic containers of all sorts, plastic beer crates, plastic bags, oil drums, dead crabs, dead fish, sheep bones, branches, shoes, polystyrene packaging, feathers . . . and seaweed.

Rushing now as I'm in the middle of a Maths practice paper. Will write properly later.

Love Duncan x

* * *

Alice helped me with the cloak. I'd already dyed the velvet curtains with navy dye so now they were darker than before and a bit streaky as if they were damp. I'd thought about machine-embroidering them with silver thread. I'd been thinking "stars", but all magicians' cloaks had stars – it wasn't very original. In fact it was a bit Harry Potter. Duncan's message got me thinking about nets. I put Mum's sewing machine on the kitchen table and started stitching silver crisscross patterns across the fabric. It looked good. That was the easy bit. The mirror pieces were more tricky.

"I thought fragments of mirror would look really cool," I said to Al. "You know, like broken shards – they'd catch the light well."

Alice was looking unconvinced. I took the mirror out of its carrier bag.

"I need to break it," I said. We took it on to the back doorstep.

"Hang on," said Al, "wouldn't it be better to break it *in* the bag – to catch the bits – or it might go in Cleo's paws." Cleopatra was sitting on the garden fence looking concerned.

"Good point," I said. I put it back in the bag and then dropped it on the step. There was a lovely smashing sound. Mum heard it from the sitting-room.

"Is everything OK?" she shouted.

"Fine," Al called back. "Isabel's just broken your best trifle dish, that's all."

"What?" Mum yelled.

"Only kidding!" Alice shouted, quickly. "Seven years' bad luck now, girl," she said, peering inside the carrier bag.

The mirror had shattered into several jagged pieces, like ice daggers. My plan was to file the sharp edges of each bit with sandpaper and then to sew the fragments on to the cloak.

It took ages. Alice cut her finger and bled on to the kitchen floor. "I hope I get a special mention in the programme for this," she said, tearing the back off an elastoplast. "Blood was shed to bring you this lavish production of *The Tempest* . . ."

I stopped at about eight o'clock, having sewn just four mirror pieces on to the blue velvet. I made a salad sandwich and took it upstairs. I was just getting going with Andrew Marvell when Jamie arrived with a box of Ferrero Rocher chocolates and a card for Mum.

"Creep," said Alice, as I passed her on the stairs.

Mum was delighted. Jamie kissed her on the cheek and (I swear!) she blushed. "Are you coming in?" she said.

"I'm sorry, I can't stop," said Jamie. "Mum's outside in the car. We're on our way back from the gym."

We went into the hallway. Mum tactfully went back into the sitting-room. Jamie smelt as if he'd just had a shower, and his hair was damp around the edges.

"It was nice of you . . . to come," I said. I kissed him – on his cheekbone, just below his left eye, and then again on the mouth. He tasted wonderful.

"See you tomorrow," he said. We were on the doorstep then, with the front door wide open. We kissed again. Hungrily. Making up for lost time. Jamie's hands danced across my back. I looped my arms round his waist and pulled his hard, fit body against me.

"God, you're so gorgeous," he whispered in my ear. He kissed the side of my neck. I moaned with pleasure.

"It's bloody draughty in here!" Pete shouted from the sitting-room.

Cheers, Pete! We pulled apart. My legs had gone all heavy, as if they wouldn't hold me up any more.

"You'd better go," I said, smiling. "Your mum's waiting."

Jamie kissed me once more, lightly, on the lips. Then he rubbed his nose against mine, eskimo kissing style. I closed the door behind him. Then I went upstairs and flopped on to my bed. My body was tingling all over. I fancied him so much!

"*I might call him a thing divine* . . ." I said out loud, quoting Miranda.

"Look at the state of you," said Alice, in the doorway.

"I'm in love!" I said, happily.

"No, you're just horny!" Alice said.

"That as well," I said, smiling like an idiot.

"You're a sad moron," Al said. She picked up a dirty sock off the floor and chucked it at me.

"Night, Alice," I said.

I was too giddy to finish my English. Sod it! It could wait. I switched off the computer, peeled off my clothes and slid under the bed covers. As I drifted into sleep I hugged the pillow as if it was Jamie, and pretended I was lying in his arms. Don't tell me I'm the first girl that ever did *that*!

Act III Scene vii

Lights up on Isabel, sitting at her computer screen in her pyjamas.

ISABEL:

I finished my English homework in the morning. I reckoned I'd skip my tutorial period and go into school a bit late – just in time for Textiles. The poem I had to write about was full of stuff about eyes and breasts and youthful skin and unsatisfied lust. Tell me about it!

I had two e-mail messages. One was junk mail trying to sell me a holiday in Tenerife. The other was from Duncan. It had been sent the night before, at ten thirty-eight.

Dear Little Miss Nosey

   Seals singing sounds like, well ... like seals singing! It's a unique sound. I can't really describe it. It's a bit like wailing, or that noise telephone wires make in the wind, or an oboe playing in its upper register, or the cries of sexual ecstasy – take your pick!

                    *   *   *

I wondered how Duncan knew about cries of sexual ecstasy. Which of his fifty-seven fellow students had he slept with – if any? That wasn't the sort of question I could ask him – even by e-mail! Safer to stick with porpoises and seaweed. I wanted to ask him if he could send us some seaweed for the set – but I seemed to be always asking for things. Now that I was going out with Jamie again I felt a bit uncomfortable about Duncan. I was worried that I was just using him. Treating him like an educational resource – a homework website. I felt like I should tell him about Jamie and me, just so he knew the score. Put my cards on the table. Then he'd know where he stood. But then he might stop writing to me – which would be sad. Very sad. Macy would say I wanted to have my cake *and* eat it. That always strikes me as a stupid saying. What's the point of having cake if you *can't* eat it?

I read on . . .

I hope you've had a nice weekend. Say "happy birthday" to your mum. Yesterday was my cousin Michael's wedding. It was in the little church at Northton. It was sunny (yes, really!) but incredibly windy. Mum's hat blew off! And the churchyard was full of sheep. Dad had to shoo them away when the photographer was taking pictures because

they kept eating the bridesmaids' flowers. I was an usher. I got to wear a tie and give out hymn books – which was thrilling, as you can imagine. Then there was a shindig at the Sebay Hotel with salmon and ceilidh dancing. I played my fiddle (did I tell you I play the violin?) in the ceilidh band. They plied us with Carlsberg Special Brew – so today I've got a bad head. I also feel strangely depressed. (Now it's my turn to get heavy!)

I've been thinking a lot about the island since I last wrote to you. You said Rimsay sounded like paradise. It *is* like paradise in lots of ways – but it's like hell too. In some ways, I can't wait to leave – to get away and escape. I know that if I go off to university next year I probably won't come back. Neil, my brother (the one who was sick on the dog!) joined the Merchant Navy and now he only comes home twice a year, when he's on leave. He's like a bird in a cage when he comes back. Of the fifteen people in his year group at school, only *one* is still on the island. All the others have gone. Flown like geese.

Michael, my cousin, and his wife Fiona got married on the island to keep my Auntie Peggy happy but they don't *live* here any more. They live on the mainland, in Glasgow. There's no future for people my age – unless you want to be a teacher in your old school . . . Which I don't!

I know Mum doesn't want me to leave. She doesn't say anything, but I can tell. I help her with Granddad and if I go, she'll be left caring for him on her own. Some days he doesn't even know who she is, and he's forever wandering off across the machair when she's at work. Dad needs me to help with the lobster fishing too. Neil used to fish a lot with Dad – he was good with boats. But now he's gone there's only me. If I could clone myself I'd leave one Duncan on Rimsay – singing to the seals – and let the other Duncan get away and get a life. (Let me know if you discover the technology, Isabel.)

Sorry to moan. How is the play? How is Prospero's cloak? And how is the lovely Jamie?

Thank you for being on the end of a modem line. Isn't cyberspace blissfully uncomplicated? Perhaps I should stay here permanently – become a virtual boy. (How sad is *that*?)

Keep smiling, love Duncan

Duncan had been honest with *me, and* he'd asked how Jamie was. So I wrote straight back . . .

Dear Duncan

Sorry you're feeling gloomy. I can see how you feel . . .

What was that word that meant feeling two things at once?

. . . ambivalent, about Rimsay. My life seems gloriously simple in comparison. I'm sure you'll make the right choices. Like you said to me: keep smiling!

You asked about Jamie . . . Jamie and I are now going out together again, and it's good. I'll bear in mind what you said about beating the crap out of him, but hopefully it won't be necessary. I think he's learnt his lesson. And he's grateful I've given him a second chance. Thanks for all the advice.

I appreciate *your* messages too. And the answers to my nosey questions! And the info about the island! And the shells! Which brings me to seaweed . . . How possible would it be for you to send me some seaweed in a parcel? (Yes, really!) I'll pay the postage of course. Not the wet slimy variety but dry stuff – the sort you'd find along the high-tide line. It would really add to the authentic island set – and we'd give you a special mention in the programme!

Time to go to school now. Shit, is that the time. I'm late!

Speak soon, love Iz x

I was late for Textiles but Miss Moss didn't mind, especially when I showed her the cloak. She really liked the mirror pieces and she let me do some more machine-embroidery during the lesson. "We'll have to photograph it," she said, "for your coursework folder."

In drama we rehearsed the storm scene. Ms Redman wants the whole cast at the side of the stage banging sheets of corrugated iron with hammers and blowing down plastic piping to sound like wind. The actors who are meant to be onboard the sinking ship – Chloe, Rosie, Phil, Jude and all the sailors – will be behind the audience, shouting into megaphones, while Prospero and I watch from the rostra tower. We have to look windswept and storm-lashed (more heads in sinks!). We look out over the audience as if they are the sea and the ship is lost in the midst of them. I thought about Duncan's cousin and wondered what happened when he drowned. What did drowning *feel* like? And what was it like to *watch* it?

"O, I have suffered with those that I saw suffer! A brave vessel, who had, no doubt, some noble creature in her, dashed all to pieces . . ." I said the lines with

real emotion. As if someone *I* knew and loved had drowned too.

It was pouring with rain when I left school, beating down in sheets. I was soaked by the time I reached the bus stop. There was a strong wind too. The bus got held up because a plastic wheelie-bin had blown into the middle of the road!

Macy came for tea. Pete cooked spaghetti carbonara.

"So, Macy . . ." Pete said. "Is this play going to be worth watching?"

"It's going to be sen-sational!" Macy said.

"Macy's great," I said. "You should hear her singing."

Macy ground black pepper on to her food with a vigorous twist of the wrist.

"Isabel wouldn't say if it had a happy ending or not?" Pete said.

Macy glanced at me and grinned.

"He needs to know how many tissues to bring," Mum said, winding spaghetti round her fork.

"I'd say . . ." Macy paused and looked thoughtful. "I'd say it was bitter-sweet."

Bitter-sweet? What did *that* mean? Was it sweet? Or was it bitter?

After tea we were looking at old photos.

"I need one of me aged about three," I said.

"Looking angelic," Macy added.

"Cherubic," I said, correcting her.

Mum has all the photographs in scrapbooks in chronological order.

"Three," Mum said, "that would be 1989 to 90." She pulled a tall spiral-bound book out of the pile.

There I was. Isabel Brownlow, aged three. Round chubby cheeks, mop of blonde hair like a dandelion clock. Isabel on Santa's knee (looking worried). Isabel on a cup and saucer roundabout at Blackpool (looking nauseous). Isabel in the garden paddling pool (looking naked!).

"That's the one!" Macy shouted. "That'll get a laugh!"

"No way!" I said, turning the page.

There I was on Dad's shoulders – Dad with his handsome face and earnest frown. Riding on Dad's back like a horse. Asleep on Dad's chest outside the Houses of Parliament. Sitting on Dad's knee pretending to drive the car.

Dad lives in Provence now, with a woman called Elise. He doesn't get in touch very often. Birthday cards – when he remembers. He's a writer – a poet. He's always skint. Skint and depressed.

Mum saw me looking at the pictures of Dad and tried to distract me. She always does that. If I try and talk about him she changes the subject. I guess she's trying to protect me – or herself.

"Over the page, there are some pictures of you on a beach in Wales. One of them might be suitable . . ." Mum said.

I flipped the pages. Alice on a horse. Mum and Dad on sunloungers by a pool. Alice dressed as Snow White. Alice and me on a tractor. And then, like Mum had said, three pictures of me on a beach – yellow bucket in hand, frilly sunhat on head. In one, I was looking at the sky. In the other, I was looking as if I was about to cry. But in the third, I was looking straight to camera with a wide, beaming smile.

"Cherubic," said Macy. "Def-in-itely cherubic!"

Miranda, aged three, building sandcastles on Prospero's island.

Once Macy started looking at the photo albums she couldn't stop. There were pictures of people she recognized from school from years ago – long before she ever met them. 1994, Sebastian Reeves dressed as a Christmas pudding in the infant play ("Like, what the hell?"). 1996, Kirsty Baker and Sara Bottomley looking like the Spice Girls at my ninth birthday party. ("As if?") 1997, Andy Shaw on a sledge.

"Cute," said Macy. "Andy was quite a sweetie when he was little. How come he's so ugly now?"

"Something happened during puberty," I said. "His face turned into a potato!"

"Poor Andy," said Mum, walking out of the room. She's always had a soft spot for Andy Shaw.

Macy was flipping pages, working her way through the pile of scrapbooks. My life in pictures. Isabel Bright, this is your life . . . Cleopatra stretched herself beside us and purred like a motor boat.

I opened the most recent album. There was me with Jamie in *West Side Story* – him in his teddy-boy suit, me in a flouncy Latin frock. On the opposite page, Jamie and me at Gran's seventieth birthday party. Jamie and me on the dodgems at the Easter Fair. Jamie and me sunbathing in the back garden. Jamie and me . . .

"Show me . . ." Macy said, looking at my dopey grin. She scanned the pages in front of me and then mimed throwing up.

I kicked her in the bum with my toe.

"You're falling for him again aren't you?"

What was the point in hiding it? I nodded.

"You're already seeing him, aren't you?" she said.

I nodded again.

"I knew it," Macy said. "You've got that helpless idiot aura about you!"

"Macy, he's different," I said. "He won't hurt me a second time. He's . . ."

Macy interrupted me. She stretched out her hand, palm towards me. "Talk to the hand, Isabel," she said. "Talk to the *hand*."

Act III Scene viii

Enter Isabel and Macy with armloads of streaky
blue clothing.

ISABEL:

Miss Moss said we could use the Textiles room at
lunchtime on Tuesday to dye some clothes. There are
big square enamel sinks in there. We ran the taps until
the sinks were full, then I emptied our carrier bags
on to a desk. We had the white jeans with the ink
stain on the knee, the bargain T-shirts and the
cheesecloth two-piece. We also had a load of cotton
sheeting that was going to be draped on the rostra
platform and used to make spare costumes. Doe had
bought cold water dye – Midnight Blue and Peacock
Blue – two lots of each. It came in little round
cannisters, like eye shadows.

"Pierce tin and dissolve powder in water," Macy
said, reading the instructions. She tried to make a hole
in the lid with her door key but it wasn't sharp enough.

"Here," I said, handing her a compass out of
my pencil case. Macy made two punctures in one
of the Midnight Blues and then lowered the tin
into the water. Two streams of dye gushed out

of the holes, making thick navy blue clouds in the sink.

"Cool," said Macy, stirring the water with a ruler. I was winding the sheeting into a long snake, twisting it together like rope and tying knots along the length of it.

"We need salt," said Macy, holding up the instruction sheet. "Four tablespoons kitchen salt for every tin of dye. What's that for?"

"To fix it," I said, "so the dye doesn't run." Mum once dyed my bedroom curtains red and when she washed them it made all Pete's underwear pink!

We'd forgotten to get salt. I rummaged in the classroom cupboards and found needles, scissors, buttons, Persil – even hot chocoate powder – but no salt.

"I'll try the food tech room," I said. I walked out into the corridor – which was a mistake. Coming towards me was Mr Horner, my French teacher. Damn! As soon as I saw him, I realized that I hadn't done his essay. I'd also missed French on Friday because we didn't get back from the Oxfam shop in time for the lesson. Doe had said she'd "smooth our path". But she's new. She doesn't know Mr Horner. He's one of those annoying teachers who think *their* subject is the only one that matters.

"Ah, Isabel," said Mr Horner. "Have you got an essay for me?"

"Sorry, sir," I mumbled. "I forgot to bring it. It's finished. Well, almost . . ." (Who was I kidding?)

Mr Horner was enjoying seeing me squirm.

"It's just," I said, "with the play . . . I'm a bit busy . . ." Bad move. Mentioning the play.

"Isabel," Mr Horner said in his most patronizing voice, "drama is only *one* of your A Level subjects. Don't you think you need to keep a sense of perspective?"

I pretended to agree with him and promised to hand the essay in first thing the next day. He smiled a greasy smile, smoothed his hair down with his hand and went on his way. I hate French. I wish I hadn't taken it.

By the time I got back with a bag of salt, Macy had wrapped all the T-shirts into neat little parcels with a ball of string and was tying pebbles into the cheesecloth skirt. I measured salt into the dye and mixed it with my hands. We put the sheet and two of the T-shirts in the Midnight Blue and the other things into the Peacock Blue. The clothes floated to the surface and bobbed there like icebergs.

"What happens next?" I said.

"Steep for one hour, stirring constantly for the first ten minutes," Macy read.

"We'll have to leave them," I said, "and come back at break."

"Or skip French again," said Macy.

"Risky," I said. I told her what Mr Horner had said.

"He's so anal," she said, with disgust. "And that thing he does with his hair gives me the creeps!"

My hands had turned blue – as if I was very cold, or dead! "Ooops," I said holding them out for Macy to see.

"Wear rubber gloves," she said, reading the instructions. "Sorry, I forgot to mention that bit!"

We went to French (worst luck) and then at break, we went back to see to the clothes. The knotted sheet was poking out of the blue water like a ghostly crocodile. I pulled the plug out of the sink and watched the inky dye sluice down the plughole. Then I turned on the cold tap and held the soggy bundles under the stream of water. It ran deep blue, then lighter blue and finally clear – like night turning into day.

"This is the best bit," I said, finding a pair of scissors and cutting the strings that held each dripping parcel. Underneath the folds – where the dye hadn't reached – were flecks of white, streaks of grey, fuzzy patches of cream cotton. It was a great effect. The garments looked like sky – and like sea too. I thought of a line Phil says as Gonzalo about *"Garments . . . being rather new-dyed than stained with salt water."*

We wrung the clothes out and pegged them on a

line beside the window, where they dripped blueish puddles on to the floor.

After school we rehearsed the love scene – Act III Scene i – the one where Ferdinand carries logs. I remembered what Duncan had said about there being no trees on Rimsay. If there were no trees on an island you'd have to collect wood from the shore for fuel – flotsam and jetsam. You'd be scavenging for every scrap of wood you could find.

"Could Ferdinand be collecting driftwood," I said, "if we're going to make the set look like the shoreline?"

Ms Redman liked the idea. I told her the beach at Ardnamurchan had been littered with wood – worn planks and broken oars and timber pallets. It hadn't, but I didn't want to tell them about Duncan. Not with Jamie standing there.

"There were loads of plastic bottles too, and oil drums and rope and netting," I said, remembering Duncan's list.

Doe got very excited about the thought of mounds of net and coils of rope lying around the stage. (I wondered if Duncan would send the seaweed.) "Excellent," said Doe. "Can you mime for now, then Jamie? Let's imagine the wood is scattered here, and here." She indicated the front of the stage – stage right and stage left.

"*Alas, now pray you, work not so hard,*" I said, clambering down the front of the rostra tower. "*You look wearily,*" I said, walking towards Jamie.

Jamie stretched and rubbed his back as if it was aching. I wished I could rub it for him. I could see a strip of tanned flesh poking out the bottom of his shirt, just above the waistband of his jeans.

"*No noble mistress,*" he said, " *'tis fresh morning with me when you are by at night . . .*" He smiled at me – big twinkly eyes, upturned mouth, lips just parted. It wasn't difficult any more to act as though I was in love with him.

"*What is your name?*"

"*Miranda . . .*"

"*O admired Miranda!*"

When we reached the end of the scene and Ferdinand said, "*Here's my hand,*" I took it eagerly. And when I pressed his hand against my heart, I wanted it to linger there, touching me.

"*And mine, with my heart in't,*" I said, stepping closer to him so he could kiss me. I could feel my heart thumping against my chest. I swallowed hard and lifted my lips up to his. Was it Ferdinand kissing Miranda? Or was it Jamie kissing Isabel? I couldn't tell any more.

"*I, beyond all limit of what else i'th'world, do love, prize, honour you . . .*" Jamie said.

"*I am a fool to weep at what I am glad of . . .*" I said. I

am a fool. *Was* I a fool? At the back of my mind –
right at the back of my mind, behind the audience,
hidden from view and barely audible – a tiny voice
told me I was. But Isabel wasn't listening. She was
too busy basking in the sunshine in her brave new
world.

Act III Scene ix

Enter Ms Redman in a blue suede jacket, closely followed by Isabel and Macy.

ISABEL:

Ms Redman asked Macy and I to go with her to the Royal Exchange Theatre to collect some stuff for the play. I love the Royal Exchange. It's like a building within a building. There's the old corn exchange – big pink marble pillars, vast domed ceiling – and all round the walls are massive black and white stills of famous actors: Vanessa Redgrave, Helen Mirren, Kenneth Branagh. Imagine having your photo up there, in the hall of fame! How cool would that be? Then in the middle of the old building there's a construction that looks like Meccano – all bright colours and tubular steel. This is the actual theatre space – in the round with seats on four sides.

There was a rehearsal in progress. Signs on the door said, "*Private. No access.*" We could hear voices – whooping sounds and singing. I peeped through a crack in a blind covering the door. There were about six actors doing a warm-up – standing with their arms stretched out. I recognized one guy from *The Bill*.

"Look," I said to Macy. She peered through the slit too. Watching them made my hair stand on end. Theatre is so exciting. I got a buzz just being there.

We went to the costume store to collect two long coats and a pair of leather boots.

"I forgot to check what size feet Jamie has," Ms Redman said.

"Tens," I said.

Macy looked sideways at me.

I pictured Jamie in the leather boots. He'd look seriously sexy.

We wandered through the props store looking for things that looked like they might have been on a ship – life-belts, ropes, rusty chain, that kind of thing. "What about a leather trunk?" I said. "Like a sea chest. Prospero and Miranda could have had their things in something like that, on the ship – all his books and stuff."

"We've got one of those at home," Macy said, "in the attic. It's my dad's."

"Do you think he'd let us borrow it?" Ms Redman said.

Macy said she'd ask.

We went downstairs into this basement where all the lights were stored. Ms Redman knew one of the lighting guys. She'd ordered six spotlight lanterns –

the stuff we've got at school is pretty basic. The guy had put them on one side for us with a label on them that said: "4 Doe."

"I've thrown in some extra cable and a couple of rolls of gaffer tape," he said, winking at her.

Ms Redman's car was parked beside the stage door. We loaded it up with all the stuff. Mr Kempe's leather jacket was on the back seat.

"What a giveaway," Macy said, out of earshot of Doe.

Ms Redman bought us lunch in the Exchange café. "We'll have missed lunch by the time we get back to school," she said.

We didn't object! Ms Redman had a salami baguette. I had a caesar salad with olive bread and a glass of cranberry juice. Every time I ate now, I remembered what Cal had said: "Actors need to be fit to move well – to push their bodies to the limits." I wanted to push my body to the limit.

"So what's Doe short for?" Macy said, as we sat down at the glass-topped table. She'd finally asked it. The question we'd all been dying to ask.

"Oh, it's pretty boring," Doe said, biting into her sandwich. "I'm really called Joanna. As a child I was Jo and then my baby brother came along and he couldn't say Jo – so he said 'Doe' and it just stuck."

"It sounds more original than Jo," Macy said. "More individual."

Listen to her, sucking up to the teacher!

Doe smiled. "Some people think it's a Homer Simpson thing," she said. "Doh!"

We laughed politely. I wondered if Macy was going to ask her if she was sleeping with Mr Kempe, now that we were on first name terms. I wouldn't have put it past her!

She didn't.

Instead, Doe turned to *me* and said, "Excuse me being nosy, Isabel, but you and Jamie, are you . . .?"

"Yes they *are*," Macy said, darkly.

"That's nice," Doe said, smiling indulgently.

"Yes," I said. "It's nice."

Act III Scene x

Isabel sits on a desk in the music room, threading shells onto a piece of string. At the piano Macy is rehearsing songs.

ISABEL:

There were no messages from Duncan on Monday, or Tuesday or Wednesday. I was beginning to worry that telling him about Jamie had been a bad move. Maybe he wasn't just a friend. Maybe he was hoping for something more – cyber romance or something! It was niggling me. Then, on Thursday, a parcel arrived in a big red van. It was a square box the size of an average TV set, all sealed up with packing tape and addressed to me.

Mum and Pete watched me open it with gaping mouths.

Inside the box were loads of crinkly black bits of seaweed – the sort you can pop like bubble wrap. Only now the bubbly bits had gone brittle and hard. There was also some long brown ropey stuff that looked like lions' tails and some feathery red bits, dried stiff like pressed flowers. That was just the seaweed. There were also four big seagull feathers, a couple of huge pink scallop shells, some blue nylon netting, a length of sandy rope, a bone that looked like it had come from a sheep's leg, and a piece of driftwood – bleached and smooth and as light as air.

I lined my treasures up along the hall carpet. Sand was scattering everywhere but Mum didn't say anything. The seaweed had a sharp salty smell.

"Wow," I said. I was amazed.

At the bottom of the box was a plastic wallet inside which was a letter and a cassette tape.

Dear Isabel

Here is some stuff from the shore. I hope you can use it. Mum thought I was mad parcelling up dirty seaweed and sending it to you!

The tape is the Posh Porpoises. I recorded our rehearsal on Monday. It sounds a bit ropey and the sound quality is awful because I was recording on a tinny little cassette player, but it gives you the idea!

Isabel, I wonder if you could do me a favour? Is there a music shop near you? I need some stuff. The only way to get it here is to order off the net and sometimes things take ages to arrive. I need some new plectrums (one fell down the gap in my bedroom floorboards and another was eaten by the goat!) and I also need a set of guitar strings – Ernie Ball Super Slinkies, if possible. I think altogether it will cost about seven quid – I'll send you the money.

I looked at the stamps on the front of the box. It had cost him nearly that much to send me all this. I could send the guitar stuff as a thank you present. I read on . . .

Sorry to moan in my e-mail the other night. I'm feeling more cheery now. The sun's shining – which helps. I got an A1 for my *Tempest* essay – so thanks for inspiring me.

I'm glad things have worked out with Jamie. I hope you didn't get in too much bother for being late for school!

All the best, Duncan x

"What a nice guy," said Mum, running her hand across the piece of driftwood.

I went into the kitchen and poured myself a bowl of muesli. Then I put the cassette in the tape player and pressed "Play". The first track was a cover version of *Yellow* by Coldplay. It was a bit rough and ready, but Duncan had a nice voice. Soulful. The next song was just starting – another cover, *Watch the Flowers Grow*, by Travis – when Pete came into the kitchen.

"Do you want a lift to school with that box?" he said. "I'm going your way if you're quick."

"Cheers, Pete," I said, gulping down the last spoonful of milk and slinging my bowl into the sink.

Macy was rehearsing at lunchtime, with Mrs Bateman, the head of Music. She's got four songs: *"Come unto these yellow sands"* in Act I Scene ii, then *"Full fathom five thy father lies"* in the same scene, *"While you here do sleeping lie"* in Act II Scene i, and *"Where the bee sucks, there suck I"* in Act IV Scene i. The first three sound quite magical – a bit weird and Bjork-like. But the last one is more jazzy, with a sleepy saxophone accompaniment. Macy's going to have big pockets with different instruments in them – a tiny xylophone, a penny whistle, sleigh bells – and she's going to play them at different places in the auditorium so the audience gets the sense that she is darting about all over the place – like a spirit, in fact.

As I listened to Macy practising, I was threading shells on a string. I'd sorted Duncan's shells into two lots. All the small ones, I'd put aside for my hair. I'd made tiny holes in them with a needle so I could thread them into my braids. They were safely zipped into a purse in my knicker drawer, ready for the dress rehearsal. But some of the shells were a bit too big. "Put those in your hair and you'll knock yourself out every time you turn your head!" Macy had said. I'd decided to make a necklace out of these ones.

When I came out of the music room, Jamie met me in the corridor. I was wearing the shells round my neck. He planted a warm kiss on my lips and ran his fingers through my hair. "Funky necklace," he said.

"It's Miranda's," I said, twiddling a mussel shell between my finger and thumb.

"It suits you," he said. He was wearing a white cotton shirt. It made him look tanned. I think he's been using the vertical tanning machine at his mum's gym. The bottom button was unfastened and I could see a patch of skin and a wisp of hair just above the waistband of his jeans. Oh, man!

"Where've you been?" he said in a sexy whisper. "I missed you."

"I was with Macy," I said, "she was practising her songs."

"Can I see you tonight?" he said, running his finger down my cheek.

"I've got to finish that French essay," I said. He looked hurt – all pouting and crestfallen. I stroked his arm. "But maybe afterwards, you could come round . . ." I said. It was Thursday – Mum and Pete's cinema night. We'd have an empty house. It was a tempting thought.

Jamie took hold of my shoulders and gently pressed me against the corridor wall. Then he kissed me again. "I can't stop thinking about you," he murmured into my ear.

Mr Horner strode past on his way from the staff room. "Not in the corridor please, Year Twelve," he barked, without stopping.

Jamie laughed. I slid my hand inside his shirt. Then Macy came out of the Music room.

"Hi," she said.

I could tell she wasn't pleased to see Jamie.

"Iz, are you still coming round tonight?" she said.

I stared at her blankly.

"To help me with my costume," she said.

I'd promised. How could I forget?

"Oh, yeah," I said vaguely. Jamie let go of my arm.

"Bring the tape, then," she said with a big grin. She bounced off along the corridor, swinging her bag on to her shoulder.

"What tape?" Jamie said.

"Just a tape Macy wants to listen to," I said, running my hand across his chest.

Jamie was looking at me suspiciously – scrutinizing my face. It made me feel . . . cornered. I remembered that feeling from before. Sort of claustrophobic. As if he wanted to keep every last bit of me to himself.

"I'll catch you later," I said.

Macy gets to wear a tight vest and combats, cut off just below the knee. Doe was worried she looked a bit butch, even though she's meant to be male. So we had this idea about pieces of gauze. We stitch all these floaty pieces of fabric to her vest and her trousers, so that when she moves they drift behind her. Then the whole thing is tie-dyed grey – streaky, smudgy.

"So it's, like, textured," Macy explained to me, sketching the idea with a pencil. "Think clouds, waves, rocks, camouflage . . . kind of elemental."

I wasn't sure it would work but I was happy to give it a try.

"And body paint on my arms and legs," Macy said, rubbing her arms. "Grey – with a touch of silver so it catches the light."

"Glitter?" I said. "On your cheekbones?"

"No," said Macy, "that's too *A Midsummer Night's Dream*. I'm a spirit of the air, not a fairy!"

"Sorr-ee!" I said.

Macy told me about this video she'd watched of *The Tempest* from the 1980s. Ariel was played by this camp bloke with an annoying voice and he wore nothing but a g-string and a load of gold body paint. "I kid you not!" Macy said. "His buttocks positively *glistened*!"

"All that glistens is not gold!" I said.

"And Caliban looked like Chewbacca from *Star Wars*!" Macy shrieked.

Andy Shaw was going to be covered in mud. Maybe we could make him a wig out of seaweed!

Macy played Duncan's tape on her bedroom music system. We were sitting on the floor, cutting two metres of gauze into pieces. It was hard to cut. It kept fraying.

"Sexy voice," said Macy as Duncan started singing an Oasis number. "He sounds like thing-a-me from the Stereophonics. I wonder if he *looks* like him too. Can't you ask him to send a photo, Iz?" she said.

"Who, the guy from the Stereophonics?" I said, being deliberately annoying.

"No," Macy said, flicking me with a piece of gauze. "Dunkin Donuts!"

"Isn't that a bit tacky?" I said. "Especially as he knows about Jamie. It's a bit like video-dating or something!"

"Say it's for *me*," Macy said, persuasively. "Say I'm curious – and single and open to offers . . ."

"No way!" I said. Now who was jealous? Now who wanted to keep things for herself! Cake and eat it! Sort your head out, Isabel!

Act IV Scene i

Lights up on the drama studio.

ISABEL:

Friday, after school, was the first full run-through of the play – although maybe "run" isn't the most appropriate word, "limp" might be a better one! Some scenes hung together OK, but overall it was a shambles. Natalie Roberts was a disaster area. She plays Trinculo, who's the king's jester, and she has several scenes with Stephano (Razia Mahmood), a drunken butler, which are *supposed* to be funny. But every time a scene gathered some sort of pace, Natalie forgot her lines and the scene lost momentum.

"Do it with the book!" Doe shouted, and someone threw Natalie a script. Forgetting lines was bad enough, but then she started corpsing (that's theatre-speak for getting the giggles during a scene).

There's this bit in Act III Scene ii where Caliban has persuaded the now-very-drunk Trinculo and Stephano to murder Prospero and take over the island. He is leading them towards Prospero's shelter to do the dirty deed, and they're jumpy because Ariel keeps spooking them with strange noises and music. Caliban says: "*Be not afeard, the isle is full of noises, sounds and sweet airs that give delight, and hurt not. Sometimes a thousand twangling instruments will hum about mine ears; and sometime voices . . .*" Those of us that aren't on stage at that point have to stand behind Chloe's painted flats and hum very softly, all on different notes. Some people have bells – like windchimes – to play very quietly to give atmosphere. It sounds really good.

Then Ariel – who's invisible – starts imitating Trinculo's voice, saying things that contradict Stephano so that it causes a fight. Stephano gets cross with Trinculo because he thinks he's telling lies (when really it's Ariel speaking) and he slaps Trinculo across the face saying, "*Take thou that!*" Natalie was supposed to turn her cheek away quickly as Razia hit her and clap her hands together behind her back so that it sounded like a really hard slap but didn't actually hurt. Natalie was too late turning her head, though, and Razia really clocked her one, so Natalie said, "Bloo-dy hell!" and everyone cracked up. After that, every time they tried the line again Natalie got the giggles. It got worse and worse until they'd been stuck at that line for about ten minutes. By then, it wasn't just Natalie corpsing, it was Razia and Andy Shaw and even Macy!

That was when Doe flipped. She'd been sitting,

cross-legged, on a chair watching the rehearsal and scribbling notes on an A4 pad. Suddenly, she hurled the notepad across the floor and yelled "STOP!" at the top of her voice. We all froze. "ENOUGH!" she shouted, standing up. "GET A GRIP!" She strode quickly towards Natalie Roberts and I wondered if *she* was going to slap her too.

But she didn't. She just fixed Natalie with a terrifying stare and said, "If it wasn't so close to the performances, I'd kick you out of this production. You've ruined every scene you've been in tonight because you're *too idle* to learn your lines." She grabbed the book out of Natalie's hands and lobbed it across the studio. "*Sebastian* knows his lines . . ." she said, pointing at Sebastian, who was leaning on the rostrum with a windchime in his hand. "*Isabel* knows her lines . . ." She gestured to me. "Andy knows *his* lines, and so does Jamie and Macy and Razia and Rosie and every flaming body except YOU!" I could see beads of spit flying out of Doe's mouth. She looked furious.

Natalie looked as if she was going to cry.

"Hasn't it dawned on you that it's under a week till our first night?" Doe said, staring round at all of us.

My stomach did a little somersault at the words "first night".

"What did I say at the beginning?" she said. She

180

didn't wait for an answer but carried on shouting. "It's all about teamwork. If one person makes a balls-up of it, they let everyone down. Like a pack of cards – one falls down, they all fall down. Natalie is letting everyone down." Natalie bit her lip. There was silence and then Doe said, "OK, from your line, '*Take thou that*!' Razia – and let's do it without the corpsing, please." Razia slapped Natalie again and Natalie delivered her reply with a stony face . . .

After the rehearsal we all sat down on the floor while Doe gave us notes. She had dozens of them scrawled across the pages of her pad. She was less smiley than usual. Brittle and tense.

"OK, general comments first . . . Well, overall – as a first run-through that was pretty crap. You don't need me to tell you that," she said. "But it had its moments. Isabel and Jamie, well done. Your scenes really worked – especially III:i. Prospero, excellent. You managed to hold the thing together – just about! Macy, lots of lovely moments, but watch your audibility." (It isn't often Macy gets told off for speaking *too quietly*!) "The Maypole dance – well, what a pig's breakfast that was! Kirsty, don't fiddle with your hair all the time . . . Isabel, watch you don't turn your back on *Brave new world* – we want to see your face . . . Rosie, don't wave your arms about so much . . ."

It was seven-thirty by the time we left school. It was pitch dark and I was starving. I texted Mum to tell her I was on the way home and needed food fast! Jamie walked me to the bus stop. We went via the eight-till-late shop where Jamie bought a bar of chocolate. I sat down on the plastic seat in the bus shelter and groaned with exhaustion.

"I thought doing plays was meant to be fun!" Jamie said, snapping off a chunk of chocolate and unwrapping the gold foil. "Reggie Clarke never used to lose it like that! She sounded like bloody Anne Robinson, the way she was talking to Natalie. What a cow!"

"It's because she wants it to be good," I said, defending Doe. "The stuff we did with Reggie was nothing like as ambitious. She's treating us like professionals!"

Jamie made a dismissive snorting noise and handed me two squares of unwrapped chocolate.

"Anyway," I said, "it pisses *me* off too, the way Natalie keeps messing up!"

"Lighten up, Izzy," said Jamie, putting his arms round me. "It's only a play!"

That's where we're different, Jamie and me. For him, it *is only* a play.

He kissed me on the nose and I smiled. I was sitting with my knees apart. He was standing in the v-shape my legs made. He stepped closer and bent his head down to kiss me on the mouth. He tasted of chocolate. I parted my lips to kiss him back. I was wearing my hipster jeans and there was a bare patch of flesh, at the back, just above my waistband, where my coat was riding up. Jamie slid his hands down my coat and rested his palms on the small of my back. Warm hands caressing bare skin. It felt good. I kissed him harder.

"I wish we could be together more, Iz," he said, brushing his lips across my cheek and nibbling my earlobe.

"We've just been together for four hours!" I said, taking hold of the lapels of his jacket and pulling him closer to me.

"No, I mean *alone*," he whispered, nuzzling his nose into the side of my neck. "So I can have you all to myself." He hooked my hair behind my ears and looked at me with that drowning look. Huge brown eyes, impossible to refuse.

I knew I needed an early night, and I had a load of French to do, plus I still had Prospero's cloak to finish, but I said, "Why don't you come round later? About nine?" And then the bus came.

After tea, while I was waiting for Jamie to arrive – after I'd had a quick bath and shaved my legs and fixed my make-up – I sent an e-mail.

Dear Duncan

Thanks SO MUCH for the fantastic parcel! You're a star! I'll get your strings and stuff tomorrow, if poss. How many plectrums do you want – and is there a special sort you want or are all plectrums the same? I've listened to about half the tape so far. I really like it. Macy thinks you sound like Kelly from the Stereophonics and she asked me to ask you to send a photo! Don't bother, if it's too much hassle! I'll write again soon.

Love Isabel x

Act IV Scene ii

Curtain opens on the Number 542 bus. It is Saturday morning, early October. There is a light coating of frost on the rooftops of West Clarendon Street. Isabel Bright, in the front seat on the top deck, holds a half-eaten Nutrigrain bar in her left hand. In her right hand she holds a mascara brush. She applies her mascara while the bus is standing still at the stop.

ISABEL:

I overslept! Macy woke me with a text message that said: *"Where R U Iz?"* I didn't have time for breakfast, or a shower – so my hair looked like greasy straw. I managed to make my eyelashes look like a drunken spider on account of the shuddering of the bus.

Jamie had stayed till half-past eleven and when he left I still had Prospero's cloak to finish – six pieces of broken mirror to stitch in place. It was nearly one in the morning by the time I'd finished. I hope Sebastian Reeves is grateful. I'd hoped to get some of the sewing done while Jamie was there – but Jamie had other ideas! Not that I minded.

I looked at myself in my make-up mirror – blue-grey eyes, freckles on nose, arched top-lip, mole on chin. Jamie kept telling me I was beautiful. I wasn't quite sure why. My eyes looked puffy from lack of sleep and I had a blackhead on the bridge of my nose that was just turning into a pimple. I daubed some concealer on it as the bus lurched away from the stop.

When I arrived at school, nothing was really happening. Everyone was sitting about drinking cans from the vending machine and Doe was talking to a guy called Jez in the Upper Sixth who's doing the lights. She was pacing about, pointing at the ceiling and looking a bit stressy. Tech rehearsals are always like that – loads of waiting around while people faff with lights and scenery. I guess that's what film and TV work is like – everyone hanging round bored rigid while the lighting crew wait for the sun to come out, or the sound man to be ready, or one of the actors to have his wig straightened. Boredom – the price of fame!

"OK," Doe said, eventually. "There's going to be a lot of sitting about today, so we all need to be patient and wrap up warm. We don't seem to have any heating yet and I don't want you all going down with flu just before our opening night . . ." (*Sudden lurch of stomach*) . . . "What we're going to do is walk through each scene of the play – not the whole scene, just the beginnings and endings and any mid-scene lighting changes or sound cues. Jez will plot each lighting change as we go and Mr Kempe will run the sound cues. That should take us till lunchtime, then we'll have a costume fitting, and while you're in costume Mr Kempe is going to take some publicity photos. Then there are some scenes I want to have a look at – especially the ones with *Natalie* in them. So Natalie, if you aren't word-perfect I suggest you take the cyanide pills now!"

Natalie smiled nervously.

"And she thinks I'm kidding," said Doe, with an ironic look. "Sonia's going to be our stage manager," Doe continued, pointing to Sonia Bogdanovich, a girl in my French group who looks like Kevin on the Harry Enfield show. "It's Sonia's job to make sure you're in the right place at the right time," Doe said. "You can use the green room and the corridor outside the studio but please come promptly for your scenes and don't leave the building without telling me."

We started the tech. Dim blue lighting for the storm. Sounds of sea crashing on beach. Flashes of white light between each of the lines of text, while we bang our sheets of corrugated iron. Then pale white light and soundtrack of distant seagulls for the opening of Act I Scene ii – the calm after the storm. Pool of light on Prospero and me ("Make sure you don't step out of the light Isabel, or your face will be in shadow . . .") getting gradually warmer as Jez brings up two floodlight lanterns with rose-tinted gels in them. Doe looked pleased. But early days yet . . .

Then came the slides shining on the back wall – Prospero, Antonio, Alonso, Gonzalo, Miranda aged three (big "Aah!") and then a surprise shot – Andy Shaw mooning from a taxi window! Everyone fell about laughing.

"How the heck did that get in there?" Doe said. She was laughing too.

Mr Kempe grinned and tapped the side of his nose.

"I'll get you, Colvin!" Andy said, flicking the Vs at Phil.

At the end of Act I Scene ii – Prospero (to Ferdinand): *"Come follow."* (To Miranda): *"Speak not to him,"* blackout – I went to the green room. The green room is a little common room at the far end of the drama studio. It isn't green, it's just called that because all actors' waiting rooms are called green rooms – don't ask me why! There are some beaten-up comfy chairs there, a giant mirror and a sofa with no arms. The whole place smells of cigarettes and greasepaint. Very theatrical.

I sat down on the sofa. Jamie sat beside me and put his arm round my shoulders. Kirsty Baker whispered something to Sara Bottomley. I bet she hates me now – now that I'm going out with Jamie again.

Macy sat on the windowsill and started peeling an orange. "Has anyone got any tapes?" she said. "For this." There was a radio-cassette player on the shelf beside the big mirror. Macy looked at me. "Iz?" she said. "Have you got that Posh Porpoises tape?"

"Posh, what?" said Andy Shaw.

"Porpoises," Macy said. "They're like dolphins."

"I know what porpoises are, Macy!" Andy said. "I just didn't catch what you said. Who are the Posh Porpoises?"

"They're a band," Macy said. "Isabel knows the lead singer."

I could see Jamie's face in the mirror opposite. He looked surprised.

"He's called Duncan," Macy said. "Dunkin Donuts!"

Was she stirring it on purpose, to make Jamie jealous? Jamie turned to look at me. I could feel myself going red.

"Who's Duncan?" he said.

Why was it such a big deal that he needed to know? I could see Kirsty and Sara whispering in a corner. Could they tell I was squirming?

"Just a friend," I said, fishing in my bag for a bottle of water.

"Friend from where?" Jamie said.

"Scotland," I said.

"Did you meet him on holiday?" Jamie said.

What if I did? He was off with Kirsty Baker at the time, wasn't he?

"He's a sort of pen-friend," I said. "He's just a mate. I've never even *met* him."

I looked at Macy, willing her not to tell them all about the message in a bottle. She got the hint and changed the subject, but then Andy Shaw said, "Well let's hear them then! The Posh Porpoises. They might be the next big thing!"

"I doubt it," I said. Reluctantly, I rummaged in my bag for Duncan's tape. Why hadn't I left it at home, out of harm's way?

Jamie took his hand off my shoulder and folded his arms in front of him. Huffy body language. I could tell he was peeved. Let him be peeved. He didn't *own* me!

Macy was putting the tape into the machine. She rewound it to the beginning and played *Yellow*.

"Nice guitar," Andy said. "Shame about the voice."

"He sounds like a Liam Gallagher wannabe," said Natalie Roberts.

"Whiney and nasal," said Jamie, looking pleased with himself. What did *he* know about it? He sings like someone out of Westlife!

Macy looked at me sympathetically. "I think he sounds sexy," she said.

"You thought that bald-headed nutter with *Ning Nang Nong* was sexy!" said Jamie sarcastically.

"This track's a bit boring," said Natalie. "Is it all like this?" Sara Bottomley was smirking.

Why did they all have to be so negative?

"Shouldn't you be learning your lines?" I said, looking at Natalie.

She gave me a dirty look. "I've learnt them, *actually*," she said.

Macy was fast-forwarding the tape. She stopped it at *Oops, I Did it Again*. There was a scream of guitars and then a thrashing drum fill.

"What the hell?" said Rosie Mason, walking into the green room.

"Britney goes mosher!" said Andy Shaw, amused.

Rosie started headbanging in front of the big mirror. "Who fancies going clubbing tonight?" she said. "We'll all need a night out after this boring crap."

I wasn't sure if by "this boring crap" she meant the technical rehearsal or Duncan's tape. I hoped she meant the rehearsal, but I never got to find out because everyone started talking about going to Music Box on the Oxford Road.

"I'm skint," said Andy Shaw.

"It's only four quid if you go before ten," Rosie said.

"I'll come," said Kirsty Baker.

Jamie wasn't saying anything. He was giving me the silent treatment. I stroked my hand across his back and fiddled with the hair at the back of his neck. That always works. I could feel his resistance melting.

"Do you fancy it?" I said, hooking my leg over his knee.

I knew Mum would kill me if I went clubbing. She keeps telling me I look washed-out and I'm trying to do too much. (Busy Izzy!) Jamie only got to stay late last night because Mum wasn't well and went to bed at half-past nine herself. I had to smuggle Jamie downstairs without Pete noticing. Luckily he was watching football with the volume right up.

I put my head on Jamie's shoulder and snuggled up to him. I could see him looking at himself in the big mirror. He reached his hand up to adjust his hair. Such a poser. But *so* gorgeous!

"Come dancing with me," I said, squeezing his knee. "It'll be fun!"

"OK," he said, turning his face towards me. I rubbed noses with him and kissed him softly.

"Yuck," said Macy, but I ignored her.

I was still kissing Jamie when Sonia called us for Act III Scene i.

"Time to go on stage," I said. "Let's go and kiss somewhere else, Ferdinand!"

"Pass me the sick-bag," Macy said, as we squeezed through the door.

The costume fitting was fun. Sebastian liked his cloak
– which was just as well as I was sick of the sight of
it. When he tried it on under the lights, the mirror
pieces gleamed and glimmered. I didn't do my hair,
but I did wear the shell necklace. And the tie-dyed
cheesecloth skirt and top and the silver velvet
waistcoat. I looked in the big mirror in the green
room. Very hippy chick. Duncan would approve.

Mr Kempe took photos of us on the set. Chloe had
found a big oil drum in a skip and some wooden
pallets. Macy had brought her dad's old sea chest.
With these and all of Duncan's bits of debris, the
set was starting to look quite authentic. Mr Kempe
photographed Jamie with an armload of driftwood,
Macy playing her penny whistle, Prospero holding
up the oar of a ship like a magic staff, Stephano
and Trinculo, staggering about drunk. Last of all he
photographed Caliban – Andy Shaw, in a cotton loin
cloth, coated all over in sticky mud.

"It's cold," Andy said, as Sonia Bogdanovich
slapped handfuls of mud on to his legs.

"You look gross!" said Macy.

"And you smell disgusting," said Phil Colvin.

"That'll be the dog poo I mixed in with it," said
Doe smiling.

"You're kidding?" said Sonia, stepping back from
the bucket.

"I'm kidding," said Doe.

"Thank God," said Andy.

After the photo shoot, Doe wanted to rehearse some scenes that I wasn't in, so I asked if she minded me going out for some fresh air. I wanted to go and get the guitar strings and stuff for Duncan. Jamie wanted to come so I had to make up a lame excuse about a secret – something for tonight.

"It's girls' business," Macy said, hooking her arm into mine. "Isn't it, Isabel?" She steered me out of the green room, winking at Jamie as we went.

The music shop is about ten minutes' walk from school. We walked fast. Because I'd overslept, I'd forgotten to check my e-mails and find out the answer to my question about plectrums. When we reached the shop there were dozens to chose from – all colours and all shapes and sizes.

"Get leopard skin ones," Macy said. "They look groovy."

"What if they're not the right sort?" I said.

"Phone him?" Macy said.

"I haven't got any credit on my phone," I said.

"Have mine," Macy said, handing me hers.

"I don't know his number," I said quickly.

"Phone directory enquiries," she said, raising her eyebrows, as if I was really thick.

I looked at her pathetically. I couldn't just *phone* him. Out of the blue. When I'd never spoken to him before.

"*I'll* phone, then," she said. She dialled one nine two. "Hello, yes, the name's Muck-Cloud ... that's MacLeod ..."

My heart started to pound. What was I so nervous about?

"What's the address, Isabel?" Macy said, holding her hand over the mouthpiece.

"Isle of Rimsay," I said. "3 The Strand, Northton, Isle of Rimsay." That tumbled out pretty easily. How come I knew it off by heart?

Macy repeated what I'd said and then she hissed, "Get a pen." I fished in my bag. "Quick," she said. I handed her a Bic biro. She wrote a telephone number down on the back of my hand and then she pressed "*End call*" and started dialling it. The number was already ringing when she handed me the phone ...

A woman answered. His mum? She had a very strong Scottish accent – which was hardly surprising.

"Is Duncan there, please?" I said.

"I'll just go and get him," she said. "Who is it?"

"Isabel," I said.

Macy was grinning at me. I could feel my heart thumping against my chest. "She's fetching him," I whispered. I looked around at all the shiny cymbals and guitars hanging from the walls. A kid with Bart Simpson hair started playing a drum kit in the corner of the shop.

"Hello," said a voice. He sounded like Ewan McGregor.

"Hi," I said. "It's Isabel."

"I know," he said. "What a nice surprise!"

"I'm in a guitar shop," I said.

"Lucky you!" he said. I laughed nervously.

"I didn't know what sort of plectrums to get," I said. My voice was trembling with nerves.

"Oh," he said, "can you get me a few? A Fender thin would be nice and maybe a Gibson – a Gibson heavy. And if they've got one, a Dunlop Flexbend as well."

"Hang on, I'll just write that all down," I said. Macy was waving a pen in front of me. "*Paper*," I mouthed, and she grabbed a leaflet about keyboards off the counter.

Duncan repeated what he'd said and I scribbled messily.

"What colour?" I said.

"Any colour! You choose," Duncan said.

"OK," I said. "And what sort of strings were they?"

"Ernie Ball Super Slinkies," he said. He sounded like he was smiling as he spoke. I tried to imagine what he looked like. Would he send a photo like I'd asked?

"I'd better go," I said. "I'm on Macy's mobile . . ."

"Say hi to Macy," he said.

"Bye," I said. I pressed "*End call*".

Macy was cheesing at me like the Cheshire Cat.

"He says hi," I said.

"What did he sound like?" she asked.

"Nice," I said, trying to sound like I wasn't bothered.

We got the stuff – exactly what he wanted. The guitar strings, and five plectrums – one fluorescent pink, one green, one silver hologramic, one leopard spotted and one tartan.

"Get tartan," Macy had said. "He's Scottish. He'll like that!"

It came to £8.50. I had just enough for a Jiffy bag and a Yorkie bar.

"I'd send him a McFlurry," I said, "except I don't think it would survive very well in a parcel!"

We walked back towards school.

"What about the surprise?" I said, suddenly remembering. "The girlie secret for tonight? What am I going to tell Jamie?"

"Tell him you went to buy condoms!" Macy said.

"Macy!" I said, in my best shocked voice.

Act IV Scene iii

The ladies' toilets, Music Box, Oxford Road, Manchester. Macy in a sleeveless silver top is applying lip gloss in the mirror.

MACY:

I know Isabel thinks I hate Jamie Burrows – and she's right, I do – and she thinks I'm always on his case, looking for stuff to criticize, but this guy has really got it coming to him. Why is Isabel so blind?

Here we are, at the Music Box. Saturday night. The place is buzzing. Packed out. We're on the dance floor – me, Izzy, Jamie, Rosie, Kirsty, Ig, Andy Shaw and Phil (looking a bit David Beckhamish in a tight white vest). It's elevenish. We're partying hard, really going for it – damp hair, rivers of sweat down the cleavage, gasping for a glass of water. You know the scene?

Then Isabel goes to the loo. She's gone a while – apparently there's a queue and she's desperate. While she's away, Jamie Burrows starts dancing with Kirsty Baker. Fair enough – we're all in a group together. But then they start to get a bit intimate – a peck on the cheek, a hand on the bum, fingers on thighs. You get the picture? I give him a filthy look and he backs off a bit. But then I spot him eyeing up a girl on the other side of the dance floor. Blonde hair, Jennifer Lopez bum, see-through top. His eyes are out on stalks. I see him saying something to Phil and they're both grinning – inching their way across the dance floor nearer and nearer to see-thru J-lo.

So he's different, is he Isabel? More mature? Eternally grateful? Eternally faithful? Bullshit!

Now, compare Jamie's behaviour on the dance floor with the sulky face on him this afternoon in the green room, and the twitchy looks he was giving Isabel when we got back from the music shop ... Isabel, spitting on the back of her hand and trying to rub out Duncan's number in case Jamie got suspicious. Isabel, making up all this crap about going to River Island for a new top and them not having one in her size. Isabel, shoving the guitar strings and the plectrums and the Yorkie Bar in a Jiffy bag – along with a letter she wrote in the girls' loos so the green-eyed monster wouldn't see – and asking me to post it for her on my way home in case Jamie looked in her bag ...

So, how come *she* can't have friends? How come she can't send a present to a mate without offending Jamie-boy?

Isabel comes back from the bathroom. She looks gorgeous. Far too good for Jamie Burrows. He's had roving hands and roving eyes but she's oblivious.

She threads her way on to the dance floor and slides her arms round Jamie's waist. He kisses her – full on, with tongues, hands dancing everywhere. When they finally come up for air, she looks insanely happy. She's smiling like an imbecile.

If only she knew . . .

Act IV Scene iv

Sunday lunchtime. Isabel, in pyjamas and pink fluffy socks, sits on her unmade bed drinking tea. Her nose is red. On the pillow are several discarded tissues.

ISABEL:

I was full of cold the next morning. Mum said it was my own stupid fault for going out late "scantily clad". She said I was over-tired. My immune system was low. That was why I'd caught whatever lurgy she'd been in bed with.

My nose was blocked. My eyes were red. When I opened my voice to speak, only a croaking sound came out. At least it was Sunday and the day was school free and (more importantly) rehearsal free. Maybe by tomorrow I'd be fine. I took some paracetamol, made myself another cup of tea, and went back to bed.

Macy woke me at about three o'clock. "You sound awful," she said.

"Thanks," I said. "That really helps."

"What if you're not better by Thursday?"

Macy's so tactful! Did she think I needed

reminding that *The Tempest* opened in just *four* days and I was bed-ridden and voiceless?

"I'll have to be better," I said.

"The show must go on!" Macy said, in a melodramatic voice.

"My public need me!" I croaked.

"Don't speak," Macy said. "You need to rest your voice."

"Well, get off the phone then," I said.

"So-rree!" she said, and then she hung up.

I sent a text to Jamie. That was the one consolation – we'd had a great night out. Jamie was *so* nice to me. And he's *so* fit. He was by far the best-looking guy in the whole place. *"Hi gorgeous! U R the best! Luv U Iz xxx"*. I sent a smiley face icon too. Just thinking about him makes me smile – even when I feel like shit!

A message came back almost straight away: *"Come and see me, sexy lady! Luv J"*. He sent a row of hearts. Bless!

I texted him again: *"Sorree can't. Am in bed."* Sad face icon.

Jamie texted me back: *"Can I come and join U?"* Smiley face icon.

"Bad idea. I'm ILL!" Sad face icon.

"O no! Get well soon". Row of flowers.

* * *

By the evening I was feeling a bit better, so I got up

and had a shower. I had some English homework that was due in tomorrow: *"Compare and contrast the sonnets of John Donne and William Shakespeare with reference to the poems on the printed sheet."* Was all English literature about sex and love, or was it just my imagination?

The computer told me I had mail – with an attachment: *"One message unread. Duncan. Subject: Mugshot!"* I clicked on the yellow envelope and it opened.

Dear Isabel

Thanks for getting the music stuff. I really appreciate it. Nice to talk in person at last rather than in virtual-speak. You sounded different from how I imagined you. Mum said you sounded polite (lots of Brownie points for that!). She calls you "the seaweed girl"!

Here is a photo for Macy – me, after winning the Rimsay under 18's table-tennis tournament. A proud moment! I scanned it from a much smaller picture so I hope it comes out OK. Just click on the paperclip and it should download.

Cheers, Duncan x

I clicked on the paperclip and the photograph began downloading bit by bit – like those mystery identity pictures on *A Question of Sport*. Duncan's hair (dark and floppy), Duncan's forehead (mostly concealed by hair) Duncan's eyebrows (dark and bushy), Duncan's eyes (smiling, like slits, creases round them, colour not detectable from photo), Duncan's nose (big – but then who am I to talk?), Duncan's cheeks (rosy and healthy-looking – islander's cheeks!), Duncan's mouth (big grin, Jamie Oliver lips, slightly crooked front teeth), Duncan's chin (goatee beard), Duncan's shoulders (broad), chest (also broad), T-shirt (blue), shorts (baggy), legs (lanky), knees (knobbly), feet (what is there to say about feet?).

There he was, filling the screen. Duncan MacLeod. I reduced the size of the image so I could see all of him at once. He was very tall. Six foot two maybe. More than six feet anyway. So I wasn't far wrong about the height. But he didn't have wild red hair and he wasn't wearing a kilt – thank God! He looked really dark – almost Mediterranean. I pressed *"Print"* and the printer whirred into action. Then I sent a quick reply:

Dear Duncan

Thanks for the picture – which I'll pass on to Macy as soon as I see her.

Congratulations on winning the table-tennis competition!

Love Iz x

I almost said he didn't look like I expected him to look (after all – *he'd* said I didn't *sound* like he expected me to sound!) but I decided against it. I didn't want him to think I'd spent hours thinking about him! That might sound flirtatious! I clicked "*Send*", blew my blocked nose, and settled down to Shakespeare's sonnets.

Act IV Scene v

Lights up on Isabel's bedroom. Isabel, in Rugrats pyjamas, is in bed, listening to music.

ISABEL:

Unfortunately, my feeling better was only temporary. When I woke up on Monday morning my head was thumping, my sinuses were blocked and I still couldn't speak. Mum made me stay off school.

"But there's a rehearsal," I said, sounding like Marge Simpson.

"Well, someone will have to be your understudy," Mum said.

I fell asleep and dreamt about the play. It was the opening night and we were in the school drama studio – only it wasn't *The Tempest*, it was *Romeo and Juliet*. I was Juliet, but I didn't know any of her lines. Romeo was Prince Charles in tights and a curly wig, but then when it came to the balcony scene, he changed – inexplicably, as is the way with dreams – into Cartman off *South Park*. The only line I knew was the one everyone knows: "*Romeo, Romeo, wherefore art thou, Romeo?*" so I said it three times. Cartman was on the other side of the stage, rummaging in a sea chest. "Where's my cheesy poofs?" he said. At that the audience started laughing hysterically and wouldn't stop. Then Doe barged on to the stage and yelled, "Get a grip!" and the audience fell silent. But that was worse than the laughter because I didn't know the next line. I needn't have worried though, because Ant and Dec appeared from the wings dressed in clown suits and riding on a motorbike, and the audience started cheering and stamping their feet. Then, thank God, I woke up!

My phone was beeping. I had a text message: "*How R U? Get well soon. Mr K woz Miranda but I didn't snog him. Luv Jx*".

I tried to imagine Mr Kempe being Miranda – with his whiskery sideburns and his leather jacket. Then I thought about Jamie – Jamie as Ferdinand, with an armload of driftwood. Jamie (or was it Ferdinand?) advancing across the stage towards me, mesmerized by Macy's singing (as if!). Jamie on Saturday night looking gorgeous on the dance floor, tasting of salty sweat and pineapple Bacardi Breezer . . .

Macy came after school with a big bunch of grapes and a pile of French homework. "You left this in the green room tape player," she said, handing me the Posh Porpoises cassette.

"Thanks," I croaked.

"Don't talk!" Macy said, holding up her hand dramatically. "Doe says you've got to rest your voice completely and drink honey and lemon with ginger root grated into it. Sounds tasty, eh? She's seriously worried about you not being well for Thursday . . ." Macy ate a handful of grapes. "Today's rehearsal was garbage," she said. "Even Sebastian sounded like he'd lost the plot."

I didn't want to know. With only three days to go, we needed to think positive – believe in ourselves. I changed the subject.

"Duncan sent you a picture," I rasped, moving my lips but hardly making any sound.

"Show me!" Macy shrieked. "Is he gorgeous?"

I pointed to a litter of paper on my desk. "It's on there somewhere," I whispered.

Macy rummaged among magazines and bits of coursework. "God, Isabel. You're so untidy," she said. "You've buried the poor guy. He should be blu-tacked to the wall . . . Aha! Who's this?" She'd found it and scrutinized the photograph. For once she was silent, then she said, "He looks like an Italian waiter!"

I stroked my chin and whispered, "It's the beard." I didn't think it worked personally. He should shave it off. But then . . . it was none of my business.

"He looks nice," Macy said. "Unsensational, but

nice. Anyway, looks aren't everything." She put the photo back on my desk.

"Keep it," I croaked. "He sent it for *you*."

"Don't *you* want it?" Macy said.

I shook my head, nonchalantly. I could always print off another copy. And anyway I'd looked at it so much it was printed in my head. Macy folded the paper and slipped it into her bag. I wondered what she'd do with it. She was disappointed. That much was obvious. It was like that moment on *Blind Date* when the screens go back and you can tell they're thinking, "Oh no, I chose the wrong one!" But I hadn't chosen Duncan. And it wasn't *Blind Date*. He was my friend. Who gave a monkey's *what* he looked like? Macy could get stuffed.

After she'd gone I played the tape. What had Natalie said he sounded like? A Liam Gallagher wannabe. Jamie had agreed. But he hadn't really meant it. He was just showing off. Being defensive.

I fast-forwarded through the Britney song. It was undeniably awful. Next was an Oasis track (which was OK) and then a noisy number called *Angry Moon* with lots of headbanging guitars. I couldn't hear the words – which was probably just as well. It was followed by a cover version of *Shining Light* by Ash. I remember that from when it was a single. Mum liked it – which is usually a bad sign! Duncan sounded good. He wasn't whiney and nasal. He was soulful and moody. This was as far as I'd listened before . . .

I let the tape run on. The next track was a quiet song that I'd never heard before. Duncan on acoustic guitar and vocals, a bit of a bassline and some soft bongos – like rain on a roof. I reached for the cassette box where Duncan had listed the tracks. It said *"Port in the Storm* – words and music by D. MacLeod"*. I snuggled under the duvet and listened to the words:

"You're my – port in the storm
You're the coat that keeps me wa-rm
You're my shel – ter . . ."

Duncan had written about boats and storms – that wasn't surprising. But who was the song about? Who was his port in the storm? Was there a girl he hadn't told me about? I pictured his face downloading bit by bit – the mop of dark hair, the laughing eyes, the big lips. He wasn't good-looking in the way that Jamie is. Jamie's got classic pop-idolish looks – symmetrical features, big eyes, neat nose, perfect white teeth. The sort of face you see on the cover of *J17* or on the bedroom walls of twelve-year-old girls. He's fit, cute, gorgeous – all those pin-up things. Duncan was – what had Macy said? – unsensational. No, that was too damning. It made him sound dull. He didn't look dull. He looked interesting.

The chorus came round again, this time with a drum fill and a haunting cello harmony: *"You're my port in the storm . . ."*

I e-mailed Duncan in the evening.

Dear Duncan

Thanks for the photo, which downnloaded no problem. Macy thinks you look Italian. I thought all Scots had red hair like the Family Ness!

I am Ill!!! Which is a disaster. I've been in bed all day drinking honey and lemon and eating grapes. I've lost my voice. Let's hope I find it before Thursday!

I like your tape and have now listened to it all – several times. My favourite song is *Port in the Storm*.

Should I ask him who he wrote it for? Maybe not.

Hope you're OK.
Love Isabel x

A message came back straight away.

Dear Isabel
I'm online doing my English homework so I

got your mail as soon as you sent it. Sorry you're not well. GET WELL SOON!

Tell Macy my ancestors are Spanish, not Italian. Apparently, in Shakespeare's time, a shipload of Spanish pirates were shipwrecked on Rimsay and they all interbred with the natives – so the story goes. Most people on Rimsay are dark-haired and a bit swarthy looking, so perhaps it's true. That would explain the madness. I'm descended from a cut-throat maniac called Carlos!

There was an attachment. I clicked on the paperclip. It was a musical greetings card. Two animated fish with straw hats and canes dancing to *Singing in the Rain* and a message that said,

"Hope the sun soon shines again. Get well soon! Love Duncan."

Act IV Scene vi

Enter Isabel, wearing a fleecy scarf and sucking cough sweets.

ISABEL:

I went into school just in time for the run on Tuesday. We were off timetable for the whole afternoon. Doe gave me a hug and said I should only talk quietly to avoid voice strain.

It was the final run-through before the dress rehearsal – without costumes or lights, but using the set and all the props. It felt flat and lifeless but we got through the whole play without any major hiccups.

Ms Redman was pleased. She said it was lacklustre and lacking in energy but all the bits were in place – there were no gaps. We were all tired and some of us were unwell – what we needed now was to go home and rest. She said the audience and the adrenalin would bring our performance to life. She'd better be right!

I spoke all my lines at half volume, and when it came to the kiss with Ferdinand I said, "You'd better not kiss me in case I'm infectious."

"Spoil sport," said Jamie with a grin. I turned my face away and he kissed the top of my head.

In the green room between scenes, Andy Shaw was scribbling on a notepad, working out anagrams of people's names. Did you know that Isabel Bright is an anagram of Gerbil Habits? Macy Paige comes out as A Cagey Imp (how apt?) and Kirsty Baker is Bakery Skirt!

We gathered on the set at the end of the run.

"OK," said Doe, smiling at us all. "Well done, you've worked really hard. I'm not going to give you any notes. Dress rehearsal tomorrow, four o'clock. Be here promptly to get into costume and make-up. I'd like to start the run by four-thirty. Off you all go and sleep! No clubbing!"

Act IV Scene vii

Wednesday, four o'clock. A sandy beach on the west side of the Isle of Rimsay. Two men – one young, one not so young – are climbing into a small boat.

DUNCAN:

Low tide was about four-thirty on Wednesday. I got out of school early to help Dad with the lobster traps. We took the boat from the bay out beyond the point and into open sea. It was a grey day. Calm, flat sea but thick drizzle hanging in the air like mist. Dad had set traps at Scarpa Rock – a long reef that lies out west, a few hundred metres off-shore. The lines were marked with buoys floating in a line, bobbing like orange footballs. We took the boat along the line of buoys, stopping at each one to haul up the traps. I was steering. Dad was operating the hauling gear, leaning out of the boat to hook the buoys with the gaff. It was a good catch. Two or three lobsters at each buoy. One or two were too small to keep so he threw them back. The others he lifted out, grasping them round their armour-plated bellies. They lunged at him with their pincers, snapping at the air.

Carefully, he banded their claws and put them in the crate in the middle of the boat. Dad was happy with the catch. He whistled as he worked, baiting the traps with mackerel and lowering them back down on to the reef.

On the way back, the wind was behind us. I opened up the outboard motor to full throttle. A grey seal was trailing the boat – dappled skin and spaniel eyes. Dad flung it a piece of mackerel off the boat floor and the seal dived under the surface and disappeared.

I thought about Isabel's play and wondered if she'd found her voice again . . .

Blackout. Lights up on the green room. Isabel sits at the mirror, wiping off make-up with a cotton-wool ball.

ISABEL:

They say, "Bad dress – good show", which is just as well as the dress rehearsal was a disaster. Everything that *could* go wrong, *did* go wrong! For a start, the storm scene was chaos. Razia Mahmood banged the piece of corrugated iron so hard, the rope it was suspended from snapped and it crashed to the floor with a deafening clatter. Meanwhile, Antonio and Gonzalo and the Boatswain (behind the audience seating) were shouting so loudly at each other that they couldn't hear each other's cues.

In Act I Scene ii, when Prospero reached inside the sea chest for his photo album, it wasn't there. So he had to mime – and then the slides jammed at the first picture of Chloe Stretton, so we saw the same slide five times over.

Caliban managed to jump a big speech by accident and cut about three pages out of the play – which made everyone else forget their lines. "If that happens tomorrow, just help each other out and try and get back on course," Doe said afterwards – as if that was the easiest thing in the world to do!

Prospero put a piece of rope round Jamie's neck on the line: "*I'll manacle thy neck and feet together . . .*" as Doe had suggested in rehearsal. Only Jamie caught his foot in a piece of fishing net, tripped and nearly choked. I rushed over to him and loosened the rope as I said, "*Sir, have pity . . .*" Jamie had tears in his eyes.

It's a wonder any of us survived the play! In the love scene, Jamie dropped a piece of driftwood on my bare foot. In the pageant, Sara Bottomley knocked the Maypole over and then got the giggles. The sea chest lid fell on Trinculo's head when he was raiding the chest for Prospero's clothes in Act IV Scene i. No one remembered to hum in the "*Be not afeard, the isle is full of noises*" scene, and we couldn't find any of the twangling instruments. "Windchimes!" said Doe to Sonia Bogdanovich, who was sitting beside her writing notes on a pad.

At the end of the play something happened to the lights, so that Prospero did his forgiveness speech in complete darkness. "Keep going Sebastian – we'll sort it . . ." Doe shouted.

Finally, the curtain jammed on our game of chess, so the audience – had we had one – would have seen nothing of us at all. When it came to my line about "*O brave new world* . . ." I had to crawl out under the curtain to say it. Sebastian almost cracked up. He had the corner of his cloak stuffed in his mouth to keep him from laughing. Such a professional!

"Everyone out front!" Doe shouted, when Sebastian had delivered his last line. Mr Kempe came out from his seat behind the sound desk and gave Doe an encouraging kiss. (Further proof – if we needed any!)

"It can't be any worse than *that* tomorrow!" he said.

In the green room, after Doe had finished giving us notes, Jamie was looking at his neck in the mirror.

"It's left a mark," he said, pulling down his collar. "Look! Like a rope burn!"

"It looks like a love bite," said Phil Colvin, taking off his bowler hat.

"I should be so lucky," said Jamie. He looked at me darkly. I was in no mood for sarcasm.

"What's that supposed to mean?" I said, throwing my waistcoat on a chair.

"Well, we haven't exactly seen much of each other, recently, have we?" Jamie said.

"I've been in bed with the flu!" I said, raising my voice. My throat was still sore and my nose kept streaming. I grabbed a handful of tissues from the make-up box and blew my nose noisily.

Kirsty Baker, hanging her costume on a rail, turned and stared at me.

"I don't just mean in the last few days, Isabel," Jamie said, pulling off his leather boots. "I mean generally. It feels like there isn't much room in your life for anyone else, Isabel – not for *me* anyway!"

"That's so unfair!" I said. I zipped up my make-up purse and threw it into my bag. I didn't need this. Not here. Not now. What was he saying? That I only thought about myself? If I stayed any longer I'd burst into tears. I grabbed my jacket off the chair and slammed the door behind me.

I was halfway home on the bus when Jamie sent a text: "*Sorry*," it said. "*Forgive me?*" Sad face icon.

Forgive me? It was so easy to say. Words were cheap. But forgiveness is as vital as air . . .

When I got home, I ran a deep bath with strawberry bubbles. I had a tune in my head. I was humming it as I ran the cold tap. I couldn't place the tune at first and then I realized what it was.

"You're my port in the storm . . ." I was singing it as I stepped into the bath and sunk into the hot foam.

Act V Scene i

Lights up on Isabel and Macy in front of a mirror. Macy is combing Isabel's hair. On the dressing table are a pile of sea shells and a bobbin of thread.

ISABEL:

I couldn't concentrate at school on Thursday. Miss Moss was merciful. She let me spend the whole of Textiles ironing costumes and putting them on hangers. Not so, Mr Horner. He had a go at me three times in French because I wasn't listening. I didn't dare make any excuses. By lunchtime the pre-performance diarrhoea had kicked in, and I spent half of English in the loo. Then it was my free period, so I went home. I was *so* fidgety. I kept looking in the mirror and saying my lines, and singing to make sure my voice was OK. I still had a bit of a cold but my voice was back – provided I didn't shout too loud. Miranda doesn't shout – which is just as well. She's far too nice. Far too mellow!

I went online – just to pass the time and take my mind off my nerves. There was a good luck message from Duncan:

221

Dear Miranda

I hope you found your voice in time for tonight.

Good luck . . . (or should I say "Break a leg"!?).

Hope it's sensational!

Love Dx

Macy came after school to do my hair. She plaited it into braids, like strands of rope, and then fastened shells on to the braids with cotton. It looked good. I wasn't sure Jamie would like it as he prefers it all floppy and dishevelled – but hopefully Ferdinand would think it looked OK. Anyway, once he's under Ariel's spell he'd fall for Miranda even if she had a bag over her head!

Mum made us some tuna sandwiches for tea, but I wasn't hungry. I picked at mine a bit and ate a satsuma. That was about all that would go down. I kept having waves of nausea and rushing to the loo. Macy doesn't seem to get nervous – or if she does, it doesn't stop her eating! She ate a huge tuna baguette and an extra-large Mars bar.

We got to school for six. Doe had set up two English classrooms just along the corridor from the studio as our dressing rooms. The clothes I'd ironed were on a hanger there, and there were some mirrors propped up on desks.

Macy and I were the first there. I did my make-up – going for the subtle, natural look – and then I helped Macy with her body paint. I was just helping her spike her hair with glitter gel when Jamie arrived. He was carrying a huge bunch of pink roses wrapped in silver paper which he handed to me with an irrresistible smile. "Ferdinand sent these for Miranda," he said. There was a card Sellotaped to the paper: "*To Miranda, I beyond all limit . . . do love, prize, honour you. Yours Ferdinand xxx*".

"They're lovely," I said. Jamie kissed me, really passionately. I felt a bit too tense to enjoy it and I was worried he'd smudge my make-up – but I didn't say anything. I didn't want him going huffy on me again. Macy didn't say anything either. She was squinting in the mirror, twisting her hair into spikes like a mad pixie.

At about quarter to seven we all went out on stage for a warm-up. Most people were in costume – apart from Andy who hadn't had his mud applied yet. The effect of all the blues and greys and smudges and streaks side by side really worked.

"You look wonderful," Doe said. "What a splendid bunch!" She was good at the cast psychology stuff. Give their egos a stroke before they go on stage. Make them feel good.

It worked. We did some stretching and arm circling and knee bending and humming. Then we all held hands in a circle. "I'm really proud of you," Doe said. "It's going to be a great show. Remember to concentrate – minds on, all the way through, whether you're on stage or off. If something goes wrong, work together to put it right and keep going. This is live theatre – you're making magic together. Do your best. Good luck!"

Jamie was standing beside me. He squeezed my hand. I squeezed it back.

It was gone seven, the audience would start arriving soon. "OK, everyone in the dressing rooms from now on please. No one out front of house," said Doe. She shook her head and her blue glass earrings sparkled.

We went backstage while Sonia and Chloe dressed the set, carefully arranging coils of rope and piles of netting and pieces of seaweed and driftwood. Jamie was still holding my hand. In the green room, Andy Shaw was telling a joke about a Rottweiler and Natalie Roberts was lighting up a cigarette. I wanted to be by myself – to prepare myself, to get "in character". I let go of Jamie's hand and said, "I'm just going to the loo."

When I came out of the toilet I didn't go back to the green room. Instead, I went along the corridor and found an empty classroom that was unlocked. I went inside and shut the door. I put my foot up on a desk and did some stretching – like I do at the bar in ballet – and some pliés in first position, then in second position ... *"Back straight, open up your shoulders ..."* Then I did some deep breathing and sang a low note, a high note, a scale, and my tea: *"Two mouth-fuls of tu-na sand-wich and a sat-sum-a!"*

"Sing through your eyes, breathe down to your feet," I told myself.

Doe says actors should always know where they've come from when they walk on stage. Where have they been before the scene starts? Who have they been with? What sort of mood are they in? Not the actors themselves, but the characters . . . I thought about Miranda. Before the storm comes and she watches the boat getting wrecked, what has she been doing?

I sat cross-legged on a desk and closed my eyes. I thought of an island – treeless, windy, flat apart from one hill. Miranda is on top of the hill. There are sheep on the hill. She is twiddling a hank of sheep's wool in her hands, plaiting it into a braid with her fingers. From the hill she can see the whole island . . . South is the sandy bay where their leaky ship washed-up so long ago – milk-white sand, studded with black rocks jutting out into the sea. West is a blow hole where the sea spouts and pops, and a line of boulders where the seals sing at twilight. North is Caliban's cave – dripping with salt water and hung with wet black seaweed. East is the shelter where she lives with Prospero – a makeshift shack built from corugated iron and salvaged wood. A washing line of salty rope. Bed covers made from torn sail cloth, pulled from the sea. And a chest full of books – old leather, water-marked, and faded clothing – velvets and brocades and fine lace – crumpled and stained and bleached by the sun. A cracked mirror, encrusted with shells and a framed picture of a woman long dead. Miranda turns and looks at the outline of the hill. Silhouetted against the pale sky she sees a golden eagle, soaring from the crags. Wind blows across her face. She stoops to pick a purple flower and threads its stem through the buttonhole of her dress. Then she looks west. Storm clouds are coming. She can see the rain out at sea, moving nearer like a dark swarm of insects. The first drops of rain fall on her face. She goes down the hill, picking her way across rough grass with her bare feet and singing to herself as she jumps from rock to rock . . .

I went back to the green room.

"Ten minute call!" said Doe. "Is everyone in make-up?"

Sara Bottomley was adding the finishing touches to Kirsty's lipstick. Sebastian was leaning against the wall, humming to himself and running lines. Macy was singing, *"Full fathom five thy father lies . . ."*

Andy Shaw was working out more anagrams.

"Did you know," he said, "that Sebastian Reeves is an anagram of Satan Bee Sievers?" He was sitting on the arm of a chair. Thick brown mud was drying on him like matt paint. "I found this website that gives you instant anagrams," he said. "You just type in someone's name and it gives you lists and lists of them."

"You sad git," said Jamie.

"Five minute call!" said Doe, poking her head round the door. "Get into your starting places and no talking on stage."

"What's the audience like?" said Sebastian.

"Quite good," said Doe. "About a hundred, maybe."

"A hundred?" said Kirsty. "Oh God!"

"Break a leg everyone," said Satan Bee Sievers.

We tiptoed into the wings and stood behind Chloe's blue and grey flats. Peeping out, I could see the raked seating filling up with people. The set was bathed in pale blue light. I could see the oil drum and a heap of seaweed and Macy's dad's sea chest. Along the edge of the front row of seating was a line of shells. Atmospheric music was playing. I could hear the buzz of audience chat. Jamie stood behind me, his arms looped around my waist, nuzzling my hair. I could feel my heart pounding against my chest.

Then the lights went down and the noise of

conversation stopped. There was silence – apart from coughing and shuffling and rustling of programmes. In the blackout, Jude and Chloe and Rosie and Phil slipped behind the audience with their megaphones, and Sebastian and I climbed the steps on to the rostra tower. There was a crash from the sound system and a flash of white light and then the banging on metal started. A cacophony of sound. Metallic clattering and strange blowing sounds like fog horns. Five seconds of noise (out of the corner of my eye I could see Doe counting in the wings, waving her arms about, one . . . two . . . three . . . four . . . five) and then some lines – shouted from the back. The audience spun round in their seats. Sebastian and I huddled on the rostra, rocking from side to side as if the wind was blowing us. Prospero in his magic cloak, holding up a wooden oar like a staff. Me, clutching a blanket round my shoulders, peering out across the sea of faces.

The storm finished – no technical hitches, thank God – and we were into Act I Scene ii. Miranda, tearful and distressed. Miranda comforted. Miranda given – at last, after twelve long years – an explanation as to why they are living on this wild, god-forsaken island. Slides working perfectly. Audience laughing in all the right places. Satisfying "aah" sound at sight of Miranda aged three, in frilly sunhat.

Then I sleep and Ariel enters: Macy bounding about the stage, on and off the rostra, telling of her magic shipwreck. Lifting a piece of driftwood above her head when she talks of the mast and pounding the oil drum with her fists when she speaks of thunder. Me waking up. Visiting Caliban. Miranda nauseated at the very thought of him. Andy Shaw crawling – monstrous and filthy – out of his cave. Prospero bullying him. Miranda calling him, *"Abhorred slave!"* Caliban spitting at us and shouting insults. (What a contrast to the Italian sophistication of the court of Milan, where serving women waited on me!) Exit Caliban.

Then Ferdinand, staggering from the sea, walking through the audience, made mad by Macy's magic song. Jamie Burrows – love of my life – wet hair, crumpled white shirt, bleached jeans, leather boots, walking towards me, smiling. Tinkling music. Macy's rich and sensual voice. Lights turning from blue to white to gold. Miranda, adoring him, thinking him indescribably beautiful, believing him utterly when he says he loves her. Moved, almost to tears – salt tears.

"This is live theatre. You're making magic together . . ."

When the lights faded at the end of Act V and we ran on hand in hand to take our bow, I was so happy I thought I'd burst. Everyone was clapping. A bunch of kids from Year Eleven were stamping their feet. We'd done it! We'd performed *The Tempest* by William Shakespeare! I was on a total high.

We all went for a drink in the King's Arms, just down the road from school. Everyone was happy. Even Andy Shaw was smiling. It felt as if we were a family. Jamie bought Macy a drink and told her she had a fabulous voice. I could tell she was pleased. I sat on Jamie's knee and he fiddled with the braids in my hair.

When I got home I sent Duncan a euphoric e-mail:

Hi Duncan
   The play was a triumph!!!!!!! I AM SO HAPPY!!!!!
   Yours ecstatically, Isabel xxxxxx

Act V Scene ii

The King's Arms, Friday night. Jamie Burrows sits, grinning, with a pint in front of him. A girl in skintight jeans is drawing with a biro on the back of his hand.

JAMIE:

The trouble with Isabel is she takes things too seriously. And she overreacts. OK, so tonight's show wasn't as good as last night's. It was raggy. We didn't concentrate so well. It was a bit flat and lifeless. A few minor things went wrong. But it wasn't a disaster. It wasn't crap. It certainly wasn't a complete disgrace.

We got off to a bad start. Natalie was mucking about during the warm-up. Ms Redman was giving her the evil eye. Then Ms Redman – or Doe, as Isabel likes to call her, which is too familiar in my opinion (teachers are teachers, not mates!) – had a go at Rosie Mason about her make-up. She'd done these wrinkle lines with eyeliner to make her look old. I reckon it looked quite effective, but Ms Redman said she looked like "bloody Spiderman".

When Sonia Bogdanovich gave us our five minute

call, Phil was in the loo which meant he wasn't in the wings during the blackout – so he couldn't get behind the audience before the lights came up. There he was, when the scene started, pegging it round the side of the stage in full view of everyone, in his Oliver Hardy hat. That would have been just about OK, if he hadn't had to run past a load of his mates who took the piss and made him laugh.

There was a crowd of Year Ten lads in the audience, all together in a gang. They laughed a lot – mostly in the wrong places. They laughed when Andy Shaw crawled out of his cave in his muddy skids, and when Prospero accused him of trying to have it away with Miranda. They laughed when Jude Lomax said Gonzalo (Phil) was an "old cock". They laughed when Chloe Stretton forgot her lines and said, "Blah! Blah! Blah! What's my next line?"

It was Phil's fault I cracked up – or "*corpsed*" as Isabel would say – in the line where I carry the wood. I'm telling Miranda that I'd do anything for her and I say: "*For your sake am I this patient log-man . . .*" As I said the word "*log-man*", I spotted Phil in the wings, trying to get my attention. He was holding this big chunk of driftwood in front of himself so it looked like a giant erect penis! Isabel's next line was, "*Do you love me?*" but I couldn't answer for laughing. Isabel was scowling at me, drilling me with her eyes. There was a pause and a few people in the audience smirked a bit. I was biting my lip, trying to stop laughing but my shoulders were shaking helplessly. Then Isabel said again, *"Well . . . do you love me?"* I managed to blurt out the next speech, avoiding looking at Phil or Iz – but I don't suppose I sounded very convincing.

Isabel's next line is the one about being a fool to weep when she is so happy. Normally she has to fake the crying, but tonight there were actually tears in her eyes. I thought it was just good acting – but maybe it was because she was mad with me. Mad, or betrayed, or humiliated. Something over the top like that!

I could tell she was mad with me, because when I kissed her a few lines later she was all stiff and she barely opened her lips. Not like her usual horny kisses . . .

She went straight to the green room after we took our curtain call and started pulling shells out of her hair and unravelling the braids. I was backstage chatting to Ig, who'd been in the audience with some of his mates from college. By the time I caught up with Isabel she was wiping make-up off her face with some greasy cream and a tissue. Her hair was all crinkly and wiggly like a Pot Noodle. I told her so, but she wasn't amused. She was giving me the silent treatment.

"Are you coming for a drink?" I said. There was a big crowd of us going down the King's Arms.

"What is there to celebrate?" she said, in a drama queenish sort of way.

"Our lurve!" I said, kissing the back of her neck. She squirmed and pushed me off with a frigid little shrug.

"It was a bloody shambles," she said. "A disgrace!"

Like I said, I didn't think the performance was *that* bad.

"I can't believe you and Phil were being *so childish*!" she shouted. On the words "*so childish*" she banged her hairbrush down on the shelf beside the mirror.

I should have read the signs but instead I made a fatal mistake. "Lighten up, Iz," I said, "it's only a play!" Only a play? Not a good thing to say to Isabel Bright – Little Miss Theatrical.

"How can you say that?" she said with a look of despair.

"I just opened my mouth and my vocal chords vibrated," I said, being deliberately annoying.

That was when she told me to go away – in language I won't repeat. I took the hint.

So here we are. No Isabel. Kirsty's keeping me company though. She's had three Bacardis – which means she's anybody's! She's sitting on my knee because there aren't enough chairs to go round. Tight jeans. Nice bum. Skimpy top leaving nothing to the imagination . . .

"Get me another drink," I shout to Phil, who's at the bar chatting up Chloe Stretton . . .

Act V Scene iii

Saturday, five o'clock. A bay near Northton, Isle of Rimsay. Duncan MacLeod, in a waterproof jacket and waders, is loading fishing gear into a small wooden boat.

DUNCAN:

I slept late on Saturday. Then I had a band rehearsal at Ned's house – or rather, in the shed that stands on the machair next to Ned's house. We rehearse there because it's miles from anywhere and we can play at full volume without annoying anybody.

It was a good rehearsal. Some of the songs were really working. Angus (our bass player) had figured out a new riff for *Port in a Storm* that sounded a bit like Radiohead. My guitar sounded great with its new strings – thanks, Isabel – and my new plecs. I cycled back along the Northton road humming to myself. It was a bright autumn afternoon. Blue sky. Low sun. Big shadows. Bracken by the roadside looking crumpled and rusty.

I got home around four. I'd promised Dad I'd help him with the traps. He'd got a special order from a hotel on the mainland. He makes a stack more money when he deals direct with the buyer, rather than selling his lobsters to the big firm who ship them off to France in a truck. I flung my bike in Dad's workshop, among boat wheels and crab traps and bits of oily dismembered motors.

Mum was in the kitchen, clattering pans. "Dad's sick," she said. "He's throwing up. Really violently. Projectile vomit. And the runs too . . ." Mum's never one to mince her words. She calls a spade a spade. "He's not fit to go out in the boat," she said.

Dad's never ill. For Mum to say he was sick he'd have to be pretty damned poorly.

They weren't keen on me going by myself.

"The forecast's not good," Dad said. He ran to the loo, clutching his belly. "It was those pies," he said between retching sounds. "I said they were past their sell-by date . . ."

"It's bright blue sky," I said, "and the wind's only light." I was outside the bathroom door shouting above the running of the tap.

I'd driven the boat often enough by myself. Sometimes I go out in summer, catching razor fish and mackerel. It was a beautiful evening. There'd be just enough daylight to get to the reef and back. No problem.

"Be careful, then," said Mum, as I packed up the gear.

"I'm always careful," I said with a grin.

I eased the boat out of the bay and round the point and then I opened the motor up to full throttle. A gannet was diving just off the starboard side – a vertical torpedo, plunging into the water with a smack, white feathers gleaming.

The first two lines were no problem. I hooked the buoys with the gaff and fastened the wires into the hauling gear. There was one lobster in the first trap – a whopper with gleaming eyes and barnacles all over its shell – and three in the second. I taped their claws with the banding tool and lowered them into the tank in the middle of the boat. Then I baited the trap, stuffing a slippery piece of herring into a twine bag (so the seals wouldn't steal it) and fastening the bag on to the bait spike. I closed the trap and lowered it gently back down on to the reef.

I was heading for the third buoy when it came on to rain. I pulled up the hood of my jacket, knotting the string with one hand as I steered the boat with my other. Out here the wind was stronger than onshore. It was coming from the south-west. I could see black clouds scudding towards me. A swell was building, lashing the boat on the portside. As I moved along the reef the waves seemed to be getting bigger.

At the third buoy, both traps were empty but the bait had gone. I re-baited the spikes and dropped them back under. The rain was coming down harder and the sky had gone suddenly dark. Thick, grey sea was bulging ominously all around me. I should have turned back at that point. Discretion is the better part of valour and all that. But four lobsters were hardly worth having. Dad's disappointed if he comes back with less than ten . . .

I turned the boat and headed for the fourth buoy. The boat was tossing badly. Surf was rolling towards it, breaking on the reef and splashing water into the front end of the boat. I had to work hard to steer a straight course, and visibility was becoming so poor I could barely see the next buoy. The wind was driving into us. Salty spray was stinging my face. When I reached the orange float and idled the motor, the boat was moving so much in the water that I couldn't hook the gaff into the eyelet in the top of the buoy. I gripped the side of the boat with one hand and reached out with the pole in the other. A huge wave came up on the port side and poured over the gunwales. When I finally got hold of the buoy with the gaff, the boat was rolling so much that I couldn't operate the hauling gear.

That was when I decided to quit and head back to the island. I turned the boat round, with difficulty, wind whipping my face. Waves were gushing over the front of the boat, swamping it and making it ride lower and lower in the water. I tried to open up the throttle to pull away from the reef, but the outboard cut out completely. It took me three attempts to restart it. By then I was completely soaked, and the waves on the starboard side were like troughs. The boat was rolling and pitching like a fairground ride. The motor spluttered into life and I opened up the throttle, just as an enormous wave came right over the boat ...

Act V Scene iv

The green room, Saturday evening. Enter Isabel, barefoot, in tie-dyed cheesecloth and a necklace of shells. She stands beside a young man in a white shirt and leather boots, seated in front of a mirror, and begins to apply make-up to his face.

ISABEL:

When I got home last night, Mum made me hot chocolate and talked to me in the bath. She'd been at both performances, Thursday and Friday. She said overall Thursday night was better, but some bits were actually *better* the second night. She said the scenes with Trinculo and Stephano were funnier and flowed better the second night and Prospero was more commanding. And she said that the audience wouldn't have known Jamie was laughing. He covered it well. "Jamie's really good," Mum said. "He's very convincing and he looks wonderful." I had to agree.

I was sorry I'd been so stroppy with him. In retrospect, perhaps I'd been a bit over the top. I wished I'd gone to the pub with the rest of them.

When I came out of the bath, I sent Jamie a text message: *"Dear Jamie, Sorry I was a bit of a cow! Call me. Iz xxxxx"*. (Sad face icon.)

He must have had his phone switched off because he didn't text me back.

I sent Jamie another message on Saturday morning: *"Dear Jamie, Do you want to come round? Love you, Iz xxxxxxxx"*.

He didn't reply. I thought perhaps he'd run out of credit on his phone. Macy came round instead and we went into town to mosey about. I had a nervous stomach. Not as bad as the first night, but still butterflies fluttering. Macy was nervous because her singing teacher was coming to the last night and all her family too.

"Dad's so critical," she said. "If he thinks it's garbage, he'll tell me – right after the show!"

"He'll think you're great," I said, reassuringly.

We were in Monsoon. There was a sale on. I was thinking of buying something new for the cast party. Doe had invited us all back to her flat after the play. I tried on a pink top. It was low-cut and frilly and flouncy in a feminine sort of way. Not the sort of thing I'd normally wear, but I reckoned Jamie would like it. He likes me in lacy, flimsy things.

"You look like Britney," said Macy, poking her head round the curtain.

"That's the idea," I said. At the back of my my mind – *right* at the back – I heard a voice – soulful, Scottish, very far away – say: "*Whatever you decide – respect yourself.*" I bought the top.

We went to Starbucks for a coffee. Cappuccino Deluxe twice with whipped cream and a double flake. I paid. Macy said she was broke.

"Imagine getting paid for doing a play," Macy said. "That would be so cool! Earning a living by acting and singing."

"Damn right," I said. Doe says I should go to drama school. She thinks I've got something special – the "X-factor", she calls it. I didn't tell Macy that, because I didn't want her to think I was showing off. But maybe she's got it too. Maybe we could go together . . .

"How's the Italian waiter?" said Macy.

"He's fine," I said, smiling. "But actually he's Spanish."

"I thought he was *Scottish*?" Macy said, dipping her finger in the cappuccino froth.

"Scottish-Spanish," I said. "An unlikely combination, I agree!"

"And damned difficult to say!" said Macy, laughing.

Alice came home especially for the play. She said she couldn't miss the chance to see her little sister treading the boards.

"Cheers, Al," I said. She was in the kitchen, making coleslaw.

"Just remember my loyalty when you're famous," she said, popping a piece of carrot into her mouth.

"So what's the verdict on tissues," said Pete. "Do I bring one or two?"

"Bring as many as you like," I said, with a grin.

"Is it sad?" said Alice, sounding surprised.

"It's bitter-sweet," said Pete, stealing a sultana from the bowl and winking at me.

I spent less time warming-up than on Thursday and Friday, because I didn't want Jamie to think I was taking myself too seriously. Anyway, now that I'd done two performances it felt easier to get into character. I felt like I knew Miranda pretty well now – we were old buddies.

I helped Jamie do his make-up, which was quite weird (and, frankly, a bit of a turn-on!). He's got lovely, soft, smooth skin. I wiped foundation across his cheeks and over his forehead, smoothing my fingers into the sockets of his eyes and down the wings of his nose. It was sensual – like modelling his face from clay.

"I could get to like this," I said.

"I'm not planning to make a habit of wearing make-up," said Jamie, and Phil laughed. I was standing with my legs astride his knees, hippy-chick skirt hitched up, bare legs brushing against Jamie's leather boots. If the green room hadn't been full of people, I'd have been tempted to ravish him – sod the make-up! I drew a fine brown line under Jamie's lower eyelid to accentuate his eyes. Such lovely eyes. Such long lashes. I kissed the top of his head.

"We missed you last night, Isabel," said Phil. "Poor Jamie was like a lost soul without you . . ." He grinned at Jamie. Jamie scowled and kicked him. I wasn't sure why.

Doe came into the green room for the ten minute call. She was looking very glamorous and sparkly. "OK, everyone," she said. "This is your last chance to get everything right. Give it all you've got. Let's make tonight the best. Complete concentration. Break several legs!"

We went into the wings. I stood behind Jamie, wrapping my arms round his waist and snuggling up behind him. Maybe I'd been a bit cool towards him lately. A bit preoccupied and tense. If he was feeling a bit neglected, maybe it was my fault. I'd show him how much he meant to me. Love changes everything . . .

I put my heart and soul into the performance. Everyone did. What had Doe said right at the start? *"We work together – everyone giving one hundred per cent – or preferably one hundred and ten!"*

The storm was electrifying. I looked out at the audience's heads, dimly lit with strange blue light, and believed for all the world that I saw waves rising and falling like watery tunnels and a boat splitting in two.

"*O I have suffered with those that I saw suffer . . .*" I said, and real tears welled up in my eyes.

When Ferdinand first appeared on the shore I cried too, overwhelmed with how lovely he looked and how miraculous he must seem to Miranda – a beautiful young man walking, unscathed, from the sea. In the log-carrying scene I kissed him enthusiastically. Then, in Act IV when we were watching the spirits' pageant, I acted as if I couldn't keep my hands off him. (Not a lot of acting required there!) Prospero has told Miranda and Ferdinand there's to be no hanky-panky and he tells them off: "*Look thou be true. Do not give dalliance too much rein . . . be more abstemious, or else, good night your vow!*" What's dalliance if not a bit of frisky snogging? So I held hands with Ferdinand and nuzzled his ears and ran my fingers through his hair and touched his knee . . . Well, we are supposed to be *engaged*!

Whenever I was offstage, I stood in the wings, entwined with Jamie, and watched the scenes in between mine. Watched Trinculo reeling drunk, watched Caliban kissing Stephano's feet and promising to be his slave, watched Ariel darting about the stage working magic, playing her twangling instruments. Why was it the last night already? I wished we could do it every night for a month . . . or a year . . . or a lifetime.

The end of the play was beautiful. When Prospero brought all his enemies into a magic circle (which Macy traced on the floor with seaweed and shells) and then forgave them, I was in tears again. What was it Duncan had said the play was about? Transformation and freedom. New starts and forgiveness and change. Things being retrieved from the sea, new-born.

Phil did Gonzalo's speech in Act V Scene i so brilliantly. *"In one voyage did Claribel her husband find at Tunis, and Ferdinand her brother found a wife where he himself was lost; Prospero his dukedom in a poor isle, and all of us ourselves when no man was his own . . ."*

I wondered if Pete was crying too.

When the lights came up, I could see Pete clapping vigorously, and Mum beside him beaming, and Alice looking proud. The seats were packed. There was our headteacher Mr Cummings, and Doe and Cal and Mr Kempe and Reggie Clarke, smiling fit to burst.

We held hands in a row and bowed for the last time as the clapping resounded around the studio. Prospero had asked for freedom from his bare island. He'd told the audience: *"Release me from my bands with the help of your good hands."* Now the play was over. The island and the storm and the magic were gone. *"Our revels now are ended . . . our actors . . . are melted into air . . . we are such stuff as dreams are made . . . let your indulgence set me free . . ."*

Lines from the play swam through my mind like darting fish. I took the shells out of my hair for the last time and put on my Britney top.

Act V Scene v

Lights up on Duncan MacLeod. Six o'clock, Saturday. The Atlantic Ocean, west of Rimsay Point.

DUNCAN:

When the first wave came across the boat, I thought we'd sink. The boat lurched to port but then it rolled back again and righted itself. I took a deep breath and looked around. The floor was flooded – gallons and gallons of water were sloshing about and ropes and fishing gear were floating like seaweed. The tank containing the lobsters was overflowing into the bottom of the boat. If I could empty it, that would lessen our weight. Once it was empty I could use the crate to bale out water before the heaviness of it pulled us under.

I switched the motor on to auto and stepped towards the front of the boat. Water was washing round my ankles. I grabbed the lobsters and hurled them into the sea – taped claws and all. Then I tried to lift the crate. It was too heavy. I started to scoop water from the surface of it with my cupped hands, frantically slopping water over the side of the boat.

Another wave broke over my head and the outboard motor cut out a second time. Now the front end of the boat was barely above the surface of the swell. Pounding waves lashed the boat, making it roll and pitch like a deranged monster. I had to grip the wooden sides to keep from being flung overboard. We were shipping water faster than ever. There was nothing I could do to stop the boat from swamping.

Suddenly a huge wave appeared on the starboard side of the boat, rising up at us like a whale breaking the surface. As it rolled towards us the boat capsized . . .

I was under the water for several seconds, my waterlogged clothing dragging me down, my waders weighing my legs down like lead. I thrashed my arms wildly, willing myself to float upwards. When my head broke the surface, I gulped in air and opened my eyes. The surface of the sea was whipped white with foam. I could see ropes flailing like water snakes, and the wires of the hauling gear, and bloody slivers of fish, slopped from the bait bucket, bobbing on the undulating water. Then I spotted the orange fuel drum – a five-gallon tank, empty and sealed – bobbing on the water a boat's length away from me. With all my strength I swam towards it and grabbed hold of the handle. Water, cold and black, was washing over my head. I gripped the tank and let its buoyancy carry me like driftwood over the heaving sea.

It was several minutes before I saw the hull of the upturned boat. The keel was rising out of the water like a dolphin's fin. I could see a length of blue rope trailing from the boat's side. Holding the fuel tank in my left hand I kicked my weary legs and propelled myself, heavily, towards the hull. With my right hand I reached for the end of the rope. It flicked and danced in the waves, just beyond my grip. Then I caught it. Thrashing my legs to keep from sinking, I managed to thread the rope through the handle of the tank and loop it round my waist. Now that the tank was lashed to my body I let go of it, and with both my desperate hands, I grabbed for the keel of the capsized boat . . .

The light was starting to fade. Wind thrashed my face and rain beat upon back. My shoulders, bobbing above the water's surface, were hunched with exhaustion. I was dizzy and confused. My hands, blue with cold and with the effort of holding, gripped the slippery boards of the boat. Deafened by the pounding roar and hiss of the ocean, I silently prayed. Prayed and waited . . .

Act V Scene vi

Enter the cast of The Tempest carrying bottles, and bags of crisps.

ISABEL:

Doe's flat was big and rambling. It was on the third floor of a vast Victorian house. We all piled in, kicking off our shoes in the hallway.

Doe had made dips and a big bowl of fruit punch. "It's non-alcoholic," she said, "I don't want to get into trouble with all your parents. *'Drama teacher supplies under-age students with drink' – shock horror!*"

Mr Kempe was searching in the cupboards for glasses. He seemed to know his way around the kitchen rather well. I helped him slop yellow punch into an assortment of glasses and plastic cups and hand them round.

When everyone had a drink, Macy tapped a spoon on the bottle of cider Andy Shaw was holding and said, "OK you guys, I think we should drink a toast ... To a great show, and a great director." We all glugged the punch. "Sonia?" said Macy with a meaningful look.

Sonia Bogdanovich stepped forward holding a big

bouquet of flowers that she'd been hiding under her coat.

Macy took them from her and gave them to Doe. "Ms Redman, these are for you as a little thank you from all of us. Thanks for a great six weeks." She kissed Doe on the cheek and gave her the flowers and a little wrapped box. The box had earrings in it that we'd all clubbed together to buy. They were amber glass – I'd helped Macy choose them in Monsoon.

"Oh, bless!" said Doe. "You shouldn't have." She unwrapped the earrings and put them on.

"Speech! Speech!" said Mr Kempe.

"OK," said Doe. "Well, I'd like to say . . . well done to all of you. You worked really hard. It was a great start to the course. Keep up the good work. You're stars – every one of you."

"Cheers, miss," Phil shouted above the clapping.

Sebastian gave Mr Kempe a six pack of beer. "These are for you, sir," he said. "For giving up all your time to help us. And we hope you'll share them with us!"

"No chance," said Mr Kempe.

"And this is for Jez," said Macy, handing over an envelope with a WH Smith voucher. "Thanks for doing the lights."

Jez smiled sheepishly. "Cheers," he said.

"Where's *my* present?" said Andy Shaw. "For

standing around covered in mud for four nights of my life!"

"You don't need a present," Macy said. "You've got the satisfaction of knowing you looked a complete prat for the cause of art."

"Did you know," said Andy, "that Piss Poor Slander is an anagram of Prospero's Island?"

"I didn't actually," said Sebastian. "But thanks for telling me . . ."

We spilled into Doe's living-room and broke into groups, chatting and eating. Macy was handing round bowls of dip and sticks of carrot and celery. Phil picked up a piece of celery and said, "What's that?"

"It's a vegetable," Macy said. "It's good for you!"

"I'll stick with cheesy wotsits," Phil said. Chloe Stretton was sitting on his knee. She'd put hula hoops on all ten of her fingers and was eating them off one by one.

Mr Kempe put on a jazz CD and Macy started dancing with him. I was chatting to Doe in the kitchen – asking her about all the theatre posters she had on the wall of the flat. Apparently she went to drama college with Kate Winslet. So why is she teaching us? I was just about to ask her that, when a tall blonde woman walked in the door. She opened the fridge and took out a bottle of tonic water.

"Isabel," said Doe, "this is Lou . . . my partner." Partner? So Macy was way out with her theories about Mr Kempe! I couldn't wait to tell her . . .

Jamie was in the lounge with Phil and Andy and a group of girls. They were laughing very loudly. Kirsty was sitting on the arm of the sofa, leaning her elbow on Jamie's shoulder. I topped up my glass with punch – laced it with a bit of the vodka Natalie Roberts had brought – and went to join them. As I joined the circle, the laughter stopped and Jamie stared at me. Kirsty gave me a strange look and got up and walked off, whispering something to Sara Bottomley.

"Did I miss something?" I said, sitting down next to Jamie and threading my arm through his. Nobody answered. I asked Jamie if he wanted to dance, but he said he wasn't in the mood. Kirsty was standing in the doorway, biting a bread stick. Jamie kept looking at her and grinning.

"What's the big joke?" I said.

"Nothing," he answered. I leaned against Jamie and ran my hand through his hair. It was all sticky and stiff with gel. He pulled away slightly and seemed irritated, so I stopped.

"Is everything OK?" I said. He'd been a bit distant all evening. Even at the play, offstage and in the wings, he'd seemed pre-occupied. Not returning my affection.

"It's fine," he said.

"Sure?" I said.

"Sure," he said.

"Are you still mad about last night?" I said. I thought we'd made up – put it behind us, new starts and all that.

"Course not," he said, smiling a bit half-heartedly. "I'm fine! Don't be so paranoid!"

"Sorry," I said. Then – foolish girl – I said, "Do you like my top?" Jamie looked at me as if he hadn't really noticed what I was wearing up until then.

"It's OK," he said, with a shrug. "It's not very *you*."

Well, that was a waste of £19.99! So much for my attempts to dress to impress! Thanks, Jamie.

I tried to start a conversation, but it was like getting blood out of a stone. "Hey, guess what?" I said. "You know Macy thinks Doe is going out with Mr Kempe? Well, I just met her partner and it's a—"

I didn't get to finish my sentence. Jamie butted in. "Do you have to talk about *Doe* all the time?" he said. He pronounced her name really sarcastically.

"How d'you mean?" I said, surprised.

"You're obsessed with her," Jamie said. "You and Macy. All that luvvie theatrical stuff. Doe this, Doe that . . . It really bugs me!"

"Sorry," I said. I felt stung. I could feel my face going red. Why was he being so nasty to me? Was he punishing me for not laughing when he corpsed or something?

"What *is* your problem, Jamie?" I said, getting off the sofa abruptly.

Ask no questions, tell no lies. If I hadn't put him on the spot, maybe he wouldn't have come out with it. But I had . . . and out it all tumbled.

"Look, Isabel," he said, "I didn't want to say this during the play . . . I didn't want to spoil it for you . . . You're a nice girl, don't get me wrong . . . It's just . . . Well, I think it was a mistake, us going out together again – thinking we could give it a second chance . . . It's just not the same is it? . . . I don't feel . . . Well, I just don't feel as strongly about you as I thought I did . . . I thought I was still in love with you, but – well, I'm not . . . Sorry . . ."

Loads of people were listening. Natalie and Phil and Kirsty Baker and Chloe. Which was worse? Being dumped by text message or by public announcement? At least he'd had the decency to wait till the final curtain call. "*Our revels now are ended . . .*" And how!

I could feel tears pricking the insides of my eyelids and my heart was battering against my chest. But I wasn't going to give them all the satisfaction of making a fool of myself. I took a deep breath and with my best acting I said, "Fine. I feel the same actually, Jamie. It was never going to happen was it?" Then I set my drink down on the coffee table, put my jacket over my stupid frilly blouse, and left.

Out of the corner of my eye, as I closed the front door of Doe's flat, I could see Macy smiling and laughing in the kitchen with Doe and Lou. I needed a shoulder to cry on, but I wasn't going to cry all over Macy. She'd say, "I told you so . . . Once a git always a git." And Alice would say the same thing. Hadn't they warned me? Hadn't they said I was a fool?

I phoned a taxi and waited on the pavement. A fat guy cruised by in a rusty car and eyed me leerily. I pulled my jacket shut across my chest and pretended to talk on the phone. Tears were coursing down my face. I wiped my eyes on my sleeve.

The taxi was a fat black one like a London cab. I climbed into the spacious back seat, feeling more alone than ever before. "West Clarendon Street, Chorlton-cum-Hardy," I said and the driver grunted and set off with a jerk.

There was only one person I could think of that I wanted to talk to. One person who would understand how I felt – who wouldn't tell me I was stupid. One port in the storm . . .

I looked at my watch. It was gone eleven-thirty. That was late to phone someone. But I was desperate. I'd stored the number the time we'd called from the music shop. I keyed in *"D"* for Duncan and the number flashed up. What if he wasn't there? What if they were all asleep and they were angry at being woken up? Damn it . . . I wanted to talk to him. Anyway, hadn't he said he'd punch Jamie's lights out if he messed me about? I pressed the call button . . .

Jamie's mum answered immediately. It was as if she'd be sitting right by the phone.

"Hello!" she said eagerly.

"Hi," I said, trying not to sound too miserable. "Is Duncan there, please?"

There was a pause and then she said, "Who's that please?"

"It's Isabel," I said. Then, remembering what Duncan had said his mum called me, I said, "The seaweed girl!"

Duncan's mum didn't answer at first. I thought we'd been cut off. Then I heard her voice, grave with emotion. "Duncan's not here . . ." she said. "He's missing . . . He went out in the boat . . . There was a storm . . . The helicopter's searching . . . I thought you were someone ringing with news . . ."

Act V Scene vii

Enter Isabel in a purple dressing gown, with crinkly hair and a tear-stained face.

ISABEL:

Mum and Pete were just going to bed when I unlocked the front door with my key. I could see the light on in their room.

"You're back early," Mum called down the stairs. I was fumbling with the lock. "Don't bolt the door. Alice is still out."

"Congratulations!" Pete shouted. "Next stop, Hollywood!"

"Mum!" I called out. My voice was shaky and thin. I dropped my bag in the hallway. Mum came on to the landing and when she saw my face she stopped smiling.

"What's happened?" she said. She ran downstairs.

"It's Duncan," I said. I fell into Mum's arms and started sobbing.

"Who's Duncan?" she said.

"The guy who found my message ... He's drowned!"

I began to cry hysterically. Mum took me into the

sitting room and made me sit down on the sofa. Pete hovered in the doorway. "Go and put the kettle on, Pete," Mum said. She handed me a box of tissues and made me tell her everything that had happened.

"But you don't *know* he's drowned," she said finally. "He might be all right. The helicopter might find him . . ." She didn't sound very convinced.

"He must have been missing hours," I wailed. "He wouldn't have gone out in the dark . . ."

He must have been missing all evening – all through the play. There we were acting out a fake storm and pretending to be sad about people drowning and Duncan was caught in a real storm. What had he said? *"Everyone on Rimsay knows someone who's drowned . . . The sea gives and the sea takes away . . ."*

Pete brought cups of tea. I drank mine down gratefully, my hands cupping the warmth of the mug.

What did it feel like to drown? To be thrown about in cold sea? To be dragged under the waves. *"Full fathom five thy father lies . . ."*

"The rescue people will find him," Pete said, optimistically. "They're ever so good . . ."

Dear Pete. Happy endings – that was what he liked. Not bitter-sweet or tragic. The future is bright, the future is Pete Bright.

I told Mum about Jamie and the cast party. It all felt utterly trivial now. There I'd been, feeling *so* sorry for myself, thinking my love life was *so* important . . . Thinking Duncan might like to hear about the trauma and heartache of Isabel Bright . . . Thinking *I* needed a port in a storm, when all along Duncan was lost at sea. Missing, feared drowned . . .

I changed out of my silly pink top and my tight jeans, and took off what was left of Miranda's make-up. My hair, where the braids had been, was frizzy and crinkled like seaweed. I looked at myself in the mirror. Less than three hours ago I'd been on stage, taking my bow, basking in the warmth of the audience's applause. Feeling invincible. Feeling like I could conquer the world. Now my adored boyfriend had dumped me twice over, and my loyal and lovely cyber-friend was almost certainly dead.

Jamie was right after all. It *is* only a play. What did Miranda and Ferdinand and Prospero have to do with real life? Prospero's Island. Piss Poor Slander.

It was five in the morning when Al came home. She'd been clubbing with some mates. She found me in the sitting-room, curled in a chair, cradling an empty cup of tea and a crumpled print-out of a guy with a big nose and a goatee beard.

Act V Scene viii

Sunday morning, six thirty-two. Lights up on an RAF Sea King rescue helicopter, flying eastwards over a calm blue sea. On board, a paramedic – female, burly arms, green overalls – checks the pulse of a young man wrapped in an inflatable suit.

PARAMEDIC:

We located the capsized boat at seven minutes past four, after a seven hour search. The vessel had drifted several hundred metres north of Rimsay Point on account of the strong south-westerly gales. We picked out the upturned hull with the search light. It was bobbing like a cork. By then, the worst of the wind had dropped but it was still a gale force six or seven. We could see what looked like an oil tank, floating by the side of the boat, but there was no sign of the missing boy. The chances of him surviving all night in weather like that were negligible. We took the helicopter down lower, just to check. That was when I spotted him. A hunched figure in blue waterproofs, tangled in a rope at the edge of the overturned hull. He looked lifeless and limp.

"Is that as close as we can get?" I said.

Jim was preparing the winch and harness. He radioed to the lifeboat which homed into view, using the beam from our lights to make its way to the capsized boat.

The boy was barely conscious when we reached him. Extreme hypothermia – uncontrollable shivering, slow pulse rate, shallow breathing, mental confusion. He was completely exhausted – stuporous. It was a tough job to winch him up without jolting him, keeping him horizontal on the stretcher to prevent a heart attack. There was a powerful downdraft from the helicopter blades, ironing the sea flat, and causing the winch cable to sway ominously. I didn't give the lad much of a chance.

Once he was onboard, we got him into the recovery position and started the thermal restablilizing. His temperature was down to thirty degrees centigrade. He was blue. We got him out of his wet clothes and into an insulating suit and put him on an IV drip. (I struggled to find a vein, his arms were so lifeless). Then we started inhalation treatment, rewarming him with warm, moist air inhaled through a mask, and we put him on a heart monitor – to check for any cardiac dysfunction.

Jim landed the Sea King on the Mull of Kintyre for re-fuelling. Then we headed for Glasgow, for Yorkhill

Hospital A&E. The wind had totally dropped and it was just getting light.

Act V Scene ix

Curtain rises on Isabel Bright and her sister Alice, standing on a station platform, overnight bags in hand.

ISABEL:

The phone rang at eight o'clock on Sunday morning, just after Alice had persuaded me to go to bed ("Four cups of camomile tea and half a box of tissues is enough for one night, my dear!") It was Duncan's mother. I ran downstairs in my pyjamas.

"They found him!" she said. "He's alive – just! They've airlifted him to Glasgow – to Yorkhill. I thought you'd like to know."

I could hardly speak. A huge lump was rising in my throat. Waves of elation were surging through me, making me feel giddy and light-headed. Duncan was alive! I thought of Ferdinand's line when he sees his father again: *"Though the seas threaten, they are merciful."*

"Thanks for ringing," I said. "It was very kind of you."

I hung up and burst into tears. Tears of relief, and exhaustion and miraculous joy. *"No more amazement. Tell your piteous heart there's no harm done . . ."*

On Sunday, Duncan's condition was described as "critical". On Monday it was "poorly but stable". By Tuesday he was "condition improving", and they moved him out of Intensive Care into a bed on the Children's Medical Ward. Now he could receive visitors, his mother said. I'd booked a ticket on the ten-thirteen train out of Manchester Piccadilly – Manchester to Glasgow, change at Preston. Three hours, fifty-five minutes.

Mum had had to talk me out of going straight away on Sunday morning. I'd have got on a train in my dressing gown, I was so keen to see him – Duncan MacLeod, pulled from the sea. My cyber pen-friend. My port in a storm. I wanted to see him, and touch him and hear his voice. We'd been *virtual* friends for long enough!

Instead of encouraging an impulsive mercy dash in Winnie-the-Pooh pyjamas, Mum sent me to bed and I slept all day. While I was asleep Macy phoned to ask why I'd left the party without telling her. "What did you say?" I asked Mum.

"I told her," Mum said.

"About Duncan?" I said.

"Of course," said Mum.

"What did she say?" I said.

"She said, 'Oh my God!' and something about donuts," Mum replied with a shrug.

Alice came with me to Glasgow. It was on her way back to Edinburgh – sort of. We caught a cab from the station to the hospital. I was nervous. First night butterflies all over again.

At the hospital, Alice tactfully went off to find the coffee bar. "You go up to the ward by yourself," she said. "I don't want to cramp your style." She winked at me as she walked off down the shiny white corridor.

There was a shop selling sweets and newspapers and bars of soap. I bought a giant Yorkie and slipped it into my bag.

Children's Medical was on the third floor. I got into the lift.

What if I didn't recognize him? What if he wasn't there? What if it was all a bizarre dream? The message in a bottle, the storm, the telephone call – everything. What if I was going mad? Too many days on Prospero's Island . . .

There was a white board at the entrance to the ward. A nurse was busy wiping out one of the names. Had that child gone home well again, or had he died? Was his mother making him chicken nuggets or weeping over a lifeless body? There was Duncan's name. Room fourteen.

I walked down the ward, peering through open doors at children surrounded by get well cards.

Children with helium balloons. Children on drips and in plaster casts. Children in cheery pyjamas.

Then I came to room fourteen. Duncan's name was on the closed door. I hesitated before opening it. Through the glass panel I could see someone propped up on a mountain of pillows. I pushed open the door.

He looked nicer than in the picture – despite being a bit pasty looking. His nose didn't look so large and the goatee beard had gone. He turned and looked at me, smiling so that his eyes creased up. I smiled back at him. *"Do you believe in love at first sight?"* *"I think it's highly likely – especially for crazy island dwellers . . ."*

After a few seconds of smiling at each other, it dawned on me that Duncan had no idea who I was. I'd seen a photo of *him*, but he'd never seen one of me. He didn't know the first thing about what I looked like. For all he knew, Isabel Bright might be five foot ten and a leggy brunette.

"Are you lost?" he said, smiling sympathetically.

"No, I'm Isabel," I said.

I didn't stay long. Duncan was still quite fragile. He said they kept talking about "core-rewarming".

"I feel like the earth's crust," he said. "They have to monitor my core temperature. You should have seen all the wires and gadgets they've had me on. I'm being gradually rewarmed. Apparently if you cool down too much you get heart failure. Hearts are pretty fragile, so it seems."

"I know," I said. I felt my eyes fill with tears. "Jamie dumped me again," I said with a sniff.

"The bastard," Duncan said. "Just wait till I get out of this bed . . ."

I laughed. "I was phoning to tell you my unhappy news when your mum told me . . . About you . . . About the storm," I said.

"Sorry I was out," he said, with a grin. "You picked a bad moment to call the e-agony aunt line. Normal service will be resumed as soon as possible!"

"I'm glad you're all right," I said. I took hold of his left hand. It felt cool. *Cold hands, warm heart.* Was it always this cool or hadn't they finished rewarming it yet? I stroked his fingers. The tips of them were ridged and hard from playing the guitar.

"They said I was lucky not to have frostbite," he said. "Can't have my fingers dropping off if I'm going to be a guitar hero."

I remembered the Yorkie. Taking it out of my bag I said, "I bought you this."

"Great," he said. "I'm on a strict diet of high energy snacks. No coffee, no alcohol, but wall to wall chocolate and glucose drops. Come in with hypothermia, go out with diabetes!"

A nurse came in and checked Duncan's pulse. Then she took his temperature and wrapped a cuff round his arm to take his blood pressure. "How're you feeling?" she said.

"Never better," Duncan said, and she grinned.

"Is this your girlfriend?" she said, glancing at me.

"You'd better ask *her*," said Duncan, smiling.

Epilogue

Enter Isabel Bright, carrying a suitcase and a McDonald's takeaway bag. She boards a small aeroplane and sits in a window seat.

ISABEL:

Now it's December the twenty-ninth. Saturday is New Year's Eve. New Year is big in Scotland. They call it Hogmanay. There's a party on the Isle of Rimsay, in the Island Centre Community Hall. There'll be ceilidh dancing and haggis and lots of whisky – and the Posh Porpoises are making a guest appearance. I'll be there to hear them.

I'm on the Glasgow to Rimsay flight. Me, the pilot and seven other people. The aeroplane is like a flying mini-bus. I'm sitting directly above the wing on the right-hand side. There's nothing to see but thick white cloud, opaque like whipped egg white. We left Glasgow an hour ago. By my calculations we should arrive in about ten minutes.

I peer into the brown takeaway bag. The Crunchie McFlurry is melting fast. By the time Duncan eats it, it will be more like a milk shake than an ice cream. But it's the thought that counts. I'm thinking about

Duncan – wondering if a week in each other's company is really a good idea, worrying that Mrs MacLeod won't like me, wondering if island folk are as mad as Duncan says they are. And I'm hoping too. Hoping the seals will be singing. Hoping the porpoises will dance beside the boat. Hoping for some island magic . . .

Suddenly we're losing altitude, falling steeply, coming in to land. I suck hard on a Polo mint to keep my ears from popping. In an instant we come out from beneath the clouds and below me I see turquoise water and green pasture and a creamy ribbon of sand binding the sea to the land. The plane turns and we head inland across lumpy grassland dotted with rocks. I can see cows and sheep and tiny white houses. Then we're at the sea again on the west side and there's a flat stretch of sand that seems to go on for ever. Traigh Mor – big beach . . .

Duncan has told me that the aeroplane lands on the beach. The tide is far out, but the hard ridged sand glistens with shallow pools. As the wheels bump down, salty spray spurts up against the window. We bounce along, sand and water flying, until the plane slows to walking pace and we coast towards a small, low building with an air sock flapping on top.

"That's the airport," says the man in the seat behind me. "Hi-tech isn't it? Welcome to Rimsay!"

I pick up my bag and step off the plane, craning my neck to keep from bumping my head on the way out. We walk across the milky sand, gleaming white shells crunching underfoot. The sun is shining brightly and the sky is fiercely blue. Wind whips my hair and plasters it across my face.

Beside the tiny terminal, Duncan is standing waiting. He wears a thick grey jumper with the neck rolled up under his chin. His eyes crinkle as he smiles at me. I walk towards him and he stretches out his arms to embrace me. As he stoops to hug me, three black cows wander through the dunes and on to the beach. Duncan clasps me to his chest just as one of the cows lets out a momentous bellow. We laugh, and with impeccable timing, Duncan says, *"Be not afeard. The isle is full of noises . . ."*

Acknowledgements

Thanks to Liz Procter for telling me about hypothermia, to Mary Kate Mackinnon (on the Isle of Barra) for telling me about *her* message in a bottle, and to my husband Tim for telling me which bits of the first draft made him laugh and cry. Also thanks to my agent Elizabeth, my editor, Emily and my sixth form drama teachers Brian and Hilary.